The Ghosts of Turtle Nest

THE GHOSTS OF TURTLE NEST

A Novel

Edith Edwards

Edith Edwards

iUniverse, Inc.
New York Lincoln Shanghai

The Ghosts of Turtle Nest

Copyright © 2007 by Edith A. Edwards

All rights reserved. No part of this book may be used or reproduced by any means, graphic, electronic, or mechanical, including photocopying, recording, taping or by any information storage retrieval system without the written permission of the publisher except in the case of brief quotations embodied in critical articles and reviews.

iUniverse books may be ordered through booksellers or by contacting:

iUniverse
2021 Pine Lake Road, Suite 100
Lincoln, NE 68512
www.iuniverse.com
1-800-Authors (1-800-288-4677)

While some characters and events in this piece may be historically accurate, this book is a work of fiction.

ISBN-13: 978-0-595-41057-6 (pbk)
ISBN-13: 978-0-595-85419-6 (ebk)
ISBN-10: 0-595-41057-X (pbk)
ISBN-10: 0-595-85419-2 (ebk)

Printed in the United States of America

Many thanks to those who read and edited the manuscript. Special thanks to members of the Writers' Bloc, Jack DeGroot, Jean Stanley, Jim Lowell, Nikki Smith, and my daughter Donna.

I'm also especially grateful to friends and family who believed and to my daughters Jana and Donna who continue to prove what strong women can accomplish.

As always, my husband Don makes it all possible.

Prologue

▼

The girl was small—Connie wondered how anyone so tiny had passed the physical. Her uniform fell forlornly around the little-girl frame. A child dressed up in soldier clothes. From beneath the camouflage cap, a frightened rabbit-face peered out at its predator. Connie smelled fear stretched skin-like between the girl and the sergeant.

"What the hell you think you're doin'?" Staff Sergeant LuElla Boggs stuck her square, stupid face into that of her prey. "I said 'Tention. 'Tention. Not show yore ass off."

"But Sarge, I ..."

"Show yore ass off. That's you, Miss Amanda Roberts, society girl. Big Daddy Senator buys his little princess into this squad 'cause ev'ry woman in America wants to help LuElla Boggs smash the Nazis in the balls. But the princess can't hack it. 'Cause Boggs don't put up with no shit. No sir."

From her stance beside Amanda, Connie saw one large tear drop onto the dusty-red Carolina soil. But the girl was quiet. She had guts. You had to give her that.

"What's the matter, Princess? Daddy ain't here to fight your battles? Take five more laps, girl. See if you can't lose that smartass crap with good, old-fashioned sweat."

LuElla Boggs turned her back as the recruit trudged onto the tarmac. "Snap to," she bawled at the other WACS. "I can't win this goddamn war with a bunch of lily-livered pussies."

After drill, Connie returned to work. As company clerk she spent hours filing, typing, making her sergeant look good.

Private Lucy McKinley, her bunkmate, was waiting for her. One of the few recruits Connie respected, Lucy was loud and boisterous, told outrageous, off-color stories, and chased men with a passion. But Connie had come to realize this uproarious personality masked a kind, compassionate soul. "Connie, please. Talk to Sergeant Boggs. She's killing Amanda Roberts, shouting at her, calling her stupid and lazy. I think she hates Amanda because she's so beautiful and comes from a wealthy family. You know we're the only unit that drills like this. Since WACS are noncombatant, it's not even expected of us. And," Lucy grinned, then winked an enormous blue eye, "if you'll help me, I'll introduce you to a certain private in Company C who is awfully lonesome."

Connie shuffled her papers and stared at her desk. "I don't think I can influence Sarge," she hedged. But she knew Sergeant Boggs berated the recruit. Petite and dainty, Amanda didn't measure up to the sergeant's idea of a WAC.

Lucy begged. "Please. Sarge'll listen to you. She will."

After Lucy left, Connie sat tapping her forehead with her pencil. Why did everyone assume she pulled strings with Sarge? Was approaching her superior even proper? Still, she enjoyed this evidence of her authority. Perhaps she could influence Sergeant Boggs. She could try.

Her opportunity came sooner than expected. That afternoon Sergeant Boggs asked Connie's opinion of the girls. "Listen to them, tell me what they say. What you think unimportant may be the key I need. I especially want to know what they think of me."

Connie felt the thrill of power. "Well," Connie hedged. "I do think moral in the unit would improve if you went a little easier on Amanda Roberts. Almost everyone feels sorry for her."

"Oh no. I don't agree with you." The sergeant grimaced. "Amanda needs toughening up. I've trained her type before. You can't baby these city girls. They get lazy if you do."

Connie shrugged. At least she'd tried.

If anything, Sergeant Boggs' harassment of Amanda became more severe. The next day at drill, Sarge separated her from the rest of the squad. Connie heard the shouts rise above drill cadence. "So, asshole. I'm too hard on you. Is that what you go whining about to my troops? Why don't you complain to Daddy? He could come down here in his limousine and take his little precious away from big, mean ole Sarge. And good riddance. We don't want no lily-livered shitfaces around here."

"But Sarge, I never ..." began Amanda.

"Of course you did. I understand that everybody feels sorry for 'Poor little Amanda.' Now shut up and get back in line. You're wasting my time." For emphasis, Sarge spattered Amanda with the sharp rocks her boot heel kicked up.

Lucy approached Connie a second time. "Since Sergeant Boggs wouldn't listen to you, some of us are meeting with the captain. And if he won't do anything, we're going to the Inspector General. Amanda needs help. She'll go bonkers if Sarge keeps messing with her mind. Come with us."

Connie considered her options. She knew Sergeant Boggs harassed Amanda and Connie pitied her. Plus she'd score coveted points with the other WACS if she accompanied them. But if Sergeant Boggs found out, which she would ... "I know everything about you girls—who's got the pip, who jerks off in bed, who's a lesbo. Don't ever lie or double-cross me. I'll make your life hell if you do." Connie knew she'd ruin her chances for promotion. And she'd be the new Amanda Roberts of the squad.

Why should she feel guilty? Didn't she join the Army for advancement? Why should she shoot herself in the foot because of a girl she barely knew? In the end, she mumbled something about finishing the day's paperwork and not betraying a superior officer.

"Please, Connie, please," Lucy begged. Lucy heard what the other recruits said about Connie—that she brown-nosed Sarge and would never defy her. But Lucy liked her, no matter what the others said.

"I'm sorry, Lucy," said Connie. "I tried once. That's all I can do."

Jilly Jones knew she shouldn't leave the barracks after lights out, but the Army food she'd eaten for supper rumbled and roiled in her stomach, making sleep impossible. She fought the battle as long as she could, then gave up and rushed for the latrine.

At full speed she rounded the shower stalls, headed for the commode. "What the ... Aaggh." A cold, clammy something slapped Jilly's face, sending her spinning onto the concrete. Shrinking from her attacker, Jilly focused her eyes, looked up, and screamed.

Swinging high above, twisting from a low-hanging support beam, was the spectral, lifeless form of Amanda Roberts. Below the corpse, an overturned chair told the rest of the story.

The purple, contorted face of the dead girl leered at Jilly as the body swung in a slow, semi-circular arc. Drawn back in a rictus snarl, Amanda's lips sagged around a protruding, swollen tongue. Her eyes bulged from the sockets, as if their owner had witnessed some unspeakable horror at the moment of death.

The paradox of the scene intensified Jilly's shock. The horror of death was juxtaposed against an almost ethereal ambience. Except for the tongue, everything about Amanda glowed with ghostly illumination—pallid skin, colorless face, even the clean bed sheet pulled tight around her neck.

But what finally overpowered Jilly, and stayed with her for the rest of her life, was the smell. The overpowering, nauseating stench of human excrement that streaked Amanda's death robe, then pooled in slimy brown puddles on the floor—the final, cleansing action of a once beautiful body.

A military hearing for Sergeant LuElla Boggs would never have taken place if a complaint had not been filed against her the day before Amanda's death. Even then, the matter might have remained hidden if Amanda's father were not United States Senator Clarence Roberts.

In the 1940s, in wartime, the Army demanded its personnel maintain sterling reputations, at least in the public eye. Americans expected value for tax dollars. Enemy governments publicized any dirty laundry as propaganda. In the Army itself, soldiers' morale deteriorated if one of their own were accused of a crime.

Captain Carl Russo considered these issues when he called for a military hearing. But he said presenting the report filed by members of Amanda's squad was his honor-bound duty. The fact that Senator Roberts visited him personally influenced that honor. "Mandy was my baby girl," bellowed an irate Roberts, blowing cigar smoke in the captain's face. "She wrote once saying she thought her sergeant treated her worse than the other recruits. Mandy never complained. And she was so proud to be a WAC. She wouldn't have killed herself if that fucking woman hadn't driven her to it.

"I blame myself, partially. I should have come down here and chewed ass as soon as I got that letter. But pressures in Washington and all, you know." For a moment, the belligerent man's mask dropped. The heartbroken pain of a father grieving for his favorite child showed in his eyes, then was gone—replaced by a flint-steel glare.

"Somebody's going to pay for this and suffer as I suffer. If you like your nice cushy duty here in the States, find out who that somebody is. Otherwise you'll be collecting enemy bullets in Germany. Do I make myself clear?" Another blast of thick smoke. Captain Russo wondered how such a small, wiry man could make himself any clearer.

Connie found herself called as a witness in a hearing for Sergeant LuElla Boggs. "I don't have any information, Captain," she protested. "I barely knew the girl."

Captain Russo disagreed. "Your position as company clerk is invaluable to us, Private Edmonds. The company clerk knows what goes on in a squad. Just tell what you saw and heard. This is not a court-martial. It's a fact-finding board, reviewing the evidence and deciding if prosecution is warranted. The people present will be you, Sergeant Boggs, a stenographer, three senior officers, and me. These are all high-ranking men, with impeccable reputations. What you say remains in strictest confidence. The courtroom will be sealed with an armed guard at the door. No part of your testimony ever leaves that room. We could subpoena you, but if you come on your own, your service record will benefit."

On the day of the hearing, Connie arrived well before her appointed time to testify. Adjusting her dress uniform, she stepped nervously into the courtroom. Sergeant Boggs' eyes drilled her as she approached the witness chair. Dreading the questions, she knew it would boil down to her desire for advancement in the Army versus her moral training. Her parents insisted on absolute truth from their children. But she was no longer a child.

Captain Russo had told her the truth. No one waited in the courtroom except the people he mentioned. The officers, two colonels, and a one-star general, conversed at the head table. The stenographer perched in front of her typewriter, efficient and impersonal. As Connie entered, Russo rose and accompanied her to the witness box. Obviously, he chaired the meeting.

"Please relax, Private Edmonds." Captain Russo administered the oath of honor and began his questioning. "I'll just ask you a few questions. Did you know Amanda Roberts?"

Beads of sweat formed at the base of Connie's scalp and trickled down her neck and starched collar. Her clammy hands knotted and unknotted in her lap.

"A little." Connie stole a glance at Sergeant Boggs, who shot pointed eye daggers in her direction. "We were in the same squad."

"Did you see Sergeant Boggs interact with Private Roberts?"

"Well, yes—in drill and in the barracks."

"Did Sergeant Boggs ever speak to Private Roberts alone in her office?"

"No." That much was true.

"Did the other girls like Private Roberts?"

"I don't know. She slept at the other end of the barracks."

"Can you think of anything, other than the military, that might have upset Private Roberts?"

Connie relaxed in her seat. She knew where Russo was leading. The Army was desperately looking for a cause for the suicide other than degradation of one of its own. Intentionally or not, Russo provided her an escape.

Crossing her long legs she drew breath. "Well ... there was this boy."

"Yes?" Captain Russo prompted.

"It's probably nothing, but she did have a boyfriend who died early in the war. Jack. Killed on the *Arizona*, as it lay docked at Pearl Harbor." Lucy had said that Amanda joined the service because of her devotion to Jack's patriotism. Connie left out the part about Amanda's pride in the boy, the Army, and serving her country.

Russo was thrilled with this new evidence. He pushed for a speedy conclusion. "Now Private Edmonds. One more question. Did Sergeant LuElla Boggs, your squad leader, ever single out Amanda Roberts by berating her, harassing her, or assigning her extra duties?"

Connie bowed her head. Deep in her soul, she knew what she would say. She made that decision the day she refused to accompany Lucy to the captain's office. Still the word stuck in her throat. "No," she finally murmured.

"I'm sorry, Private Edmonds. Would you repeat your answer so the whole court can hear?"

Connie raised her head. Telling the partial truth about the boyfriend made the second lie easier. Her green eyes flashed as she made eye contact with the captain. Crossing an undefined threshold she declared, "No. No, I never did."

There. Finished. For the first time in her life she had told an absolute lie. Connie didn't know if she was relieved or ashamed. She just wanted out of that courtroom. If Russo harbored any more questions, he wouldn't get answers from her. She stood, and without another word, fled the scene.

Sergeant Boggs returned to the unit. Russo told Connie that the court had dropped charges against her due to lack of evidence. The sergeant and Connie avoided each other whenever possible. Within a month Boggs was transferred from the squad. The new sergeant brought her own clerk. Connie rejoined the rank and file.

In November Connie received a disturbing note. She found it lying on her bunk in a plain, white envelope. The handwriting broadcast boldness and self-assurance. Masculine writing, she assumed. Connie shuddered when she read it.

I know what you did at the trial. I'm gathering evidence. I'll contact you soon.

The handwriting and tone threatened her peace of mind. She thought she was finished with Amanda's death and the hearing. Who wrote such a note? Russo had promised secrecy. She knew no one in the courtroom sent it.

After receiving the note, Connie noticed that the girls in her squad shunned her more than ever. Now hostility replaced simple avoidance. Connie sensed barely-concealed hatred from the others. Conversations halted when she entered a room. Angry eyes followed as she carried out her daily chores.

When she thought about it, she traced this reaction from her squad members to the day she received the menacing note. But how could the recruits know the contents of the message?

Lucy remained Connie's one friend. By nature, Lucy believed everyone possessed her kind and generous soul. But she was puzzled. "I don't understand, Con. How come Sergeant Boggs wasn't court-martialed? She caused Amanda's death. I know you can't talk about the hearing, but it's strange."

On December first a shiny, gray limousine glided to a stop in front of squad headquarters. The recruits wondered what important person visited their sergeant. Not a military man. Not in that car.

The company clerk stomped into the barracks and summoned Connie. "Sarge wants you."

"What for?" Connie had never talked to the new sergeant, much less entered her office.

"How the hell do I know? I deliver information. I don't make it." The girl shot Connie a look of hatred similar to the glares she received from other recruits. She slammed out the door without waiting for Connie.

At company headquarters the new sergeant and a short, intense-looking man confronted Connie. "Private Edmonds," the sergeant began, "this is Senator Clarence Roberts, Amanda Roberts' father. He thinks you can shed some light on …"

Senator Roberts interrupted the sergeant. "Actually, I hope you can help me with my grief, Private Edmonds. Amanda was my baby. I'm talking to everyone who knew her."

The sergeant did not appreciate the interference. Her voice iced as she continued. "Senator Roberts wants you to go for a drive. I could refuse, but we cooperate with civilians. I told the senator you may take a short ride with him."

The diminutive man gripped Connie's arm with surprising strength. She was pushed forward, ushered to the door before she could protest.

"Thank you, lieutenant." Senator Roberts elevated the sergeant several ranks. "Your assistance will be remembered."

"Just bring her back soon. And I'm a sergeant, not a lieutenant."

Senator Roberts' driver opened the limo door. Except for the firm grip, the senator assured Connie's comfort as he helped her into the car. After the door slammed, his mood changed.

"Why'd you lie? Why'd you lie in the courtroom?" Some people considered Clarence Roberts handsome. Now his well-chiseled features sharpened with rage.

"What?"

"Why'd you tell that captain Amanda killed herself because of a boy? Why'd you say LuElla Boggs didn't mistreat her?" Senator Roberts drew a Churchill cigar from his coat pocket and contemplated it. Methodically placing it on the flat surface of his briefcase, he retrieved a double-bladed cutter and chopped the head off the stogie with one efficient, guillotined-style movement. After lighting it, he puffed in silence, staring straight ahead. The car slowly filled with smoke.

Connie's thoughts were in turmoil. *How did Roberts know what took place at the hearing? Russo promised secrecy. This man knew everything.*

Roberts turned to face her, blowing smoke. "You thought I didn't know. Ha. Knowing what goes on is my business. Especially when my family or my business interests are concerned."

Connie could hardly breathe. Dense, nauseating smoked filled her lungs. "P-please put down a window," she begged.

"Uncomfortable, huh? Think how uncomfortable my little girl was with that asshole sergeant on her all the time." The senator leisurely blew two smoke rings before lowering the window. They rode in silence until the smoke cleared.

"Is that better? Then remember this. I know what you did. And I can make your life miserable. I *will* make your life miserable. I've already started. Have you noticed that the girls in your squad hate you? That's because one of them received a letter telling the truth about you. Only Lucy Shumate remains loyal.

"Don't confess. I own a transcript of exactly what was said in that courtroom. LuElla Boggs escaped court-martial, but believe me, she's not happy in her new duty station. I've made certain of that. She may not be with us much longer, rest her soul."

"You. You sent the letter, didn't you? You, or someone who works for you."

The edges of the senator's thin lips curled upward. He delayed so long in answering that Connie didn't think he would. "That letter is one of many you'll get for the rest of your life. Letters, phone calls, robberies, lost promotions—all bad.

"Whenever anything unpleasant happens, look over your shoulder. You'll see Clarence Roberts. I maintain contacts throughout the state, throughout the country. My control stretches a long, long way. You may never set eyes on me again, but you'll feel my influence for the rest of your life. Yes. Even after I die. I possess that much power."

Without Connie realizing it, the senator had signaled for return to the barracks. Roberts said no more. He appeared mentally withdrawn from the scene. After the limousine pulled to the curb, the driver manhandled her from the car. The big machine sped away, cigar smoke trailing from the rear window.

CHAPTER 1

▼

THWARTED AGAIN

1977

"Damn. Damn." Connie slammed the phone into its cradle. She couldn't believe it. For the third time her petition appeared to have failed. Her sources in Raleigh were telling her that the votes were not there to permit her to develop Turtle Nest—her project on a barrier island off the coast of Southport, North Carolina. Clarence Roberts at work again. Eighty-five years old, long retired and out of Washington, he still thwarted her plans.

She'd worked so hard putting this package together. The owners agreed. The environmentalists were satisfied. The state legislature had been well lobbied. Now this. She snatched up a notepad headed "Edmonds Real Estate and Development Co—We Sell the Beach" and wrote SHIT, SHIT, SHIT!

She could not evade Roberts' tactics. Connie laid her head on her desk, cradled in her forearm, and remembered. *Amanda Roberts, pretty, petite daughter of Senator Clarence Roberts, berated and harassed by Sergeant Luella Boggs. Thirty-two years ago, World War II, we had been WACS. Sergeant Boggs hated Amanda because of her beauty and family connections. Lucy, another WAC, had begged for help. As company clerk, I could talk to Sergeant Boggs. If that didn't work, we would seek out the ombudsman. I refused. I wanted to advance in the Army. That didn't happen if you antagonized your superiors. Finally, Amanda could take no more. One night she had hanged herself in the latrine. I testified at the hearing. Said I'd never seen Sergeant Boggs humiliate Amanda.*

"I lied," Connie whispered.

Clarence Roberts had laid the blame on Connie. He had promised to make the rest of her life miserable. He fought as she opened her business, sabotaging every move. Potential buyers avoided property because of false rumors of drainage problems, legal entanglements, or Connie's "questionable" integrity. In spite of Senator Roberts, she had made her real estate business the finest in Southport, maybe in the whole southeast and enjoyed a reputation as an honest, reliable land developer.

Connie was tired—tired of fighting Roberts, tired of obstacles everywhere she turned, tired of working every day. Once her job challenged her. Now it weighted her with duty and boredom. Locating property for a potential buyer, interaction with her staff, even taking care of her own home—things that had once given her pleasure—had become hated responsibility.

As she sat at her desk, she began slipping. Slipping into that horrible place to which her spirit fled much too frequently these days. Try as she might, she could not hold onto reality. She felt like a seashell, washed ashore, desperately clinging to the sand while being sucked back into the great void of the ocean. She clenched her fists in a futile effort to avert approaching danger. She knew what came next.

Wave upon wave of inertia washed over her. Though awake, she was bolted to her chair by an invisible force. Somewhere in the back of her head something jangled, a bell, no, metal—maybe coins—rattled together in annoying disharmony.

The jangling in her head intensified until it became a force of its own. Connie's body shook from the reverberation. Still she had no control of her will. She sat immobile until the sound consumed her. Then it stopped abruptly, leaving emptiness more menacing than the sound itself.

She lay limp across her desk, unable to move. Her limbs were stiff and heavy, drugged from the onslaught of the nightmare. Finally, she yielded to the lethargy and sank into semi-consciousness.

Some time later—she had no idea how much later—her secretary Maggie knocked, then entered. "Goodness, what are you doing sitting here in the dark?" she asked, switching on the lights. Connie blinked in confusion, a dull throb pounding somewhere behind her eyelids.

Maggie ignored Connie's red eyes and puffy face. Her employer had been acting strange lately. She often seemed confused and disoriented. Maggie had trained herself to stick to business and not interfere. Connie became hostile if questioned.

Using her best professional voice, Maggie said, "Lucy James is in the outer office. At least, I think her last name is James this month."

The awful sluggishness lifted and Connie's spirits rose. "Give me a minute, Mags. Let me make myself presentable, then show her in." Connie didn't realize her mood swings were obvious to her staff.

Dear Lucy. She had remained a friend for over thirty years. Lucy was on husband number three. Or was it four? She'd lost count. Connie hadn't seen Lucy in over a year, but communicated with her often. She had received an invitation to Lucy's most recent wedding. The ceremony had taken place in Hawaii, on the beach. Always exotic. Lucy never changed.

Lucy entered the room and held out her arms. She still sported the girlish figure and wild black hair of her years as a WAC. Only her eyes told that she had suffered—and matured. Trusting innocence had abandoned the purple irises, for—what? Confidence, surely, but another quality. Something akin to "You can push me so far, but no farther."

This perception of Lucy played through Connie's mind as she crossed the room and hugged her friend. Lucy smelled of face powder and rose water. Lucy returned the hug, then looked closely into Connie's face. "Hey. What's with you? You look like someone rained on your parade."

Connie threw up her hands in frustration. "Someone did. But I'm not dwelling on that now. Not with you here. Lucy, you're still as trim as when we were WACS. And what a beautiful outfit." Lucy's polyester trouser suit with bell-bottom pants, macramé vest, and platform shoes were the height of fashion.

"I bought it for my honeymoon. Or at least to wear on the plane to Hawaii. Didn't wear too much *after* the ceremony." Lucy winked that flirtatious wink that Connie remembered well.

"I bet. Sit down. Tell all. It's so good to see you! What are you doing in Southport? Why didn't you tell me you were coming?"

Lucy crossed the elegant room and chose a Chippendale wing chair. Before sitting, she admired the view of the harbor. "Lovely. You've made quite a name for yourself, Connie. I'm here to see you, of course. And ask for money."

Connie laughed. "What's your scheme now, Lucy?" She might as well get straight to the point. Lucy obviously didn't need money for herself, but she was always championing a cause. Last year it was saving baby seals. Though Connie teased, she admired her friend's energy. When Lucy supported an endeavor, she attacked it with single-mindedness. Today proved no exception.

"St. Bettina's Episcopal Church needs remodeling," Lucy said. "It's one of the oldest churches in North Carolina, and it's falling down. St. Bettina's existed during the Revolution but it won't be with us much longer if it keeps on deteriorating."

"Aw, Luce. You know I'm not a religious sort." *And harbor no intentions of changing my mind*, thought Connie. She sat across from her friend in the matching wingback.

"Maybe you should reconsider," mumbled Lucy.

"What did you say?"

"Nothing." Lucy hesitated. "It's just that maybe you should become involved in a church. You succeed at everything. You've met all your goals. But the time may come when you need more. We're not getting any younger, you know."

"No thanks." Exasperated, Connie twirled a strand of hair. "Churches contain hypocrites. Senator Clarence Roberts claims to be a religious man, but he's the biggest fake of all."

In spite of her vow to forget Roberts, Connie found herself filling Lucy in on her business problems. "It's a beautiful island, Luce. Our development will be right at the base of Old Baldy, the lighthouse. We've named it Turtle Nest because the Loggerheads lay eggs there, deep in the sand. Roberts' argument hinges on development hurting the environment, especially the turtles. I disagree. We can't halt growth. But we can control change—assure it's well planned, rather than haphazard.

"And North Carolina is ready for a development like this. South Carolinians have Hilton Head. Floridians vacation at Palm Beach. We need an upscale resort in this state. But I've rattled on. I'm sorry. Tell me about Charlie, or is it Bob?"

Lucy's laugh tinkled across the room. "It's Charlie. Bob was husband number one. This one's for keeps. He's so good to me." She flashed the large diamond on her left hand. "We're only in North Carolina briefly, then we sail to Bermuda."

Lucy stared at the ring, then raised her eyes to her friend. Gathering courage, she launched the conversation in a new direction. "The other reason I'm here, and perhaps the most important, is to tell you about Charlie. Or rather, to tell you about the changes in my life because of him."

Connie sighed. She cared little for honeymoon drivel. But Lucy's next words were far from drivel.

"As you know, Charlie's my fourth husband. This time it will work. I'm going to make it work. I met Charlie in a bar, of all places. He wanted to marry the next week. I knew right away he was special, but I couldn't get married that soon.

"You see, there's part of my life you know nothing about. I've done a good job of hiding it, even from myself. When I met Charlie I had begun seeing a therapist. Still am, as a matter of fact. It was either that or go to the detox unit at the county jail."

Connie sat straight up. "Lucy. I had no idea."

"No one did. I became an alcoholic, suffering through three bad marriages. I was a mess. I told Charlie I wouldn't marry him until I straightened out my life."

Lucy stood and crossed to the large bay window. Yachts from up and down the eastern seaboard were moored at the docks. Beyond, barely visible in the ocean, she watched as ships from all over the world plied their slow, steady journey to the port in Wilmington. Sunlight, unfathomable blue-green water, brave birds diving for their dinner, gave her strength to continue.

"That's what I want to share, Connie—what the therapist helped me understand. He made me realize I let some really nasty things happen because of feelings from long ago. Feelings about Amanda Roberts' suicide."

"But Lucy. That was over thirty years ago." The Roberts thing again. Connie grew weary of dealing with that family.

"To my subconscious, it happened yesterday. My counselor helped me see that I felt guilty. Guilty Amanda died. Guilty I couldn't prevent it. The girls in the squad looked up to me. Considered me a mother figure. Yet I couldn't save one of my own."

"You tried. If anyone tried, you did."

"But I failed. Amanda still died. Maybe there was something else I could have done. In retrospect, I should have contacted her father. Anyway, that's the tape my psyche played year after year. So much so it convinced me I was a bad person, not worth being loved or taken care of.

"That's why I tortured my body and hooked up with three losers. My first husband abused me, verbally and physically. The other two were just worthless. Couldn't hold a job and ran around with other women. Once I came home and found my third husband and his honey in our bed. I had affairs, too. I sank pretty low before being arrested for drunk driving and being forced to see a therapist. It was my third DUI offense."

Connie toyed with the Limoges figurine beside her chair. How could this be? Thirty years and she'd had no clue that her friend was suffering. Yet she'd rarely seen Lucy during that time, and then only briefly. Their friendship had continued through Christmas and birthday cards, a quick letter, an occasional telephone call.

"But you always sounded so cheery when you called. And sent such funny cards and notes."

Lucy shrugged. "According to my counselor, that's part of it—failing to admit there's a problem. That's the way these bad feelings operate. They can only hurt you if they stay hidden. But when brought to the light of day, you see them for what they are. Lies and innuendoes. Then their vicious power vanishes. So I'm here partly for my own healing and partly for yours."

"Mine? I'm not sick." Connie ducked her head. She was unwilling to admit, even to herself, that these slips into semi-consciousness were becoming more frequent.

"I don't mean to pry, Connie. Believe me, it's difficult opening old wounds. But we've been friends a long time and I care about you. Truth is Connie, I worry about you. Lately you seem changed when I telephone—distant, removed. You're not the Connie I've known for thirty years.

"We were so young when Amanda died. Only eighteen. And the suicide affected our lives, whether we knew it or not. Maybe you haven't even realized its effect on you. But consider it. It almost killed me. Maybe you should talk to someone."

"Oh, Lucy." Connie waved her hand in dismissal. "I can't worry about that. Sure, it shook me up at the time. But it happened so long ago. I'm perfectly healthy. And there's enough going on in my life right now. My business keeps me occupied. I can't dredge up things from the past. If a problem surfaces, I'll deal with it. I can't pay someone to listen to my drivel."

She wasn't mad at Lucy. How can you censure a grown woman who reminds you of Tinkerbell? The conversation unsettled her, though. Lucy's troubles were one thing. She regretted her friend suffered bad marriages and lost years. But her life concerned no one but herself.

Lucy had expected little more from Connie, spending years in denial herself. Still, she felt she must try. "Think about it, Connie. Old memories hang around like death shrouds. You may need to dredge them up—for your own sanity."

Connie frowned. "My only problems with Amanda Roberts are the ones her father cause me right now. He halted the Turtle Nest project with his political influence. At least for the next few years. I just wish I could make those politicians see the beauty of the island, and the benefits of developing it."

Lucy thought a few moments, then her face lit up. She flew across the room and pulled Connie from her chair. Twirling Connie in a crazy dance, she squealed with excitement. "That's it. You've solved it. You must make the legislators see the island. I'm sure you've told them about it, shown them pictures. But they need a first hand view. Maybe you could take a few politicians over there. Better yet, take them all. Have a business meeting on Turtle Nest, or a party. Yes. Definitely a party. Invite the old buzzards—and their wives. Get them in a good mood, relaxed and well-fed, then hit them with your sales pitch."

"Oh, I don't know, Lucy. It wouldn't work. And I'm tired of dealing with it."

"Hey, that's not the Connie who just told me she dealt with her problems. It would work. If there's one thing politicians like, it's a party—at someone else's expense."

"It's over, Lucy. Roberts has won, at least for the time being. I can't fight him anymore."

"But you must. Don't you see?" Lucy slammed her fist into her palm to emphasize her point. "Isn't Amanda's death still haunting you? If you give in now, Roberts wins. A party's a great idea. It could turn the tide on the vote in the legislature."

"Well—I don't know. It might work." Connie's down-turned lips showed her doubt. "I could ask my staff what they think."

"Do that. They'll be all for it."

They chatted another half hour, catching up on their respective lives. Lucy left with a promise of a $500 pledge for St. Bettina's. Connie admitted that one reason she gave that much was so Edmonds Development Company could be listed as a gold donor in the newspaper. That mattered little to Lucy. The old church needed all the support it could get.

After Lucy left, Connie rehashed the conversation. She never imagined Lucy had led such an unhappy life. She'd met the first three husbands, though briefly. All were handsome and charming. Connie had envied Lucy's luck with men. Now she didn't envy her at all. What a nightmare. Lucy had succeeded in keeping her life a secret. Thank goodness things had improved. Charlie James sounded like a jewel.

But imagine—Lucy suggesting a therapist. *Hmmpf.* She could take care of her own problems, thank you. Only the weak needed a shrink. Funny. She'd never thought of Lucy as weak.

After hearing Lucy's story, Connie decided it didn't matter that she'd never met the right man. She'd assumed she'd marry and have children. She'd wanted children. Now she was too old. Anytime an affair threatened commitment, she began to label the man insipid or frighten him off with her business success or intelligence. And Connie had also sensed fear on her part. She'd even had nightmares of something, or someone, blocking closeness between her and any man she dated.

Connie swiveled her chair to overlook the Southport harbor and shook off these depressing thoughts. This was her meditation space. Many business problems had been solved by the tranquility of boats swaying on their moorings or the flash of the lighthouse across the inlet.

Her vision of pristine beaches, upscale homes, condominiums and a clubhouse seemed doomed. She, the architects, and her able staff had worked long hours planning, designing, creating. Accessible only by water, a ferry would shuttle people and goods back and forth to the island. No cars would be allowed. The historic lighthouse, Old Baldy, remained the focal point of the village. An old post office and a nondenominational church would be refurbished. Any new structures would blend with those already in place and with the landscape.

Best of all, the developers had assisted biologists in preserving the environment. Buyers were ready for this. Because of images sent from the moon landing, the country realized that the earth is an interdependent, life-supporting system. Now, since the oil crisis of 1973, public opinion was beginning to demand conservation.

Turtle Nest would become a haven for all wildlife—especially the giant Loggerhead sea turtles. The females could make their slow, arduous journey ashore to lay their eggs without disturbance.

As Connie watched, three brown pelicans swooped across the horizon. The last one stopped to dive bomb a fish he spotted in the waves. *I love pelicans,* she thought. *They're not beautiful, but they're so gutsy. A few years ago, I never saw a pelican. Since the pesticides that destroyed their eggs were outlawed in 1973, they're coming back. They'll thrive on Turtle Nest.*

Connie was proud that in addition to wildlife protection, Edmonds Development Company had devised extensive plans safeguarding the dunes and marsh. Sea oats, with their long, golden stalks, would be planted for stabilization of the beach. Workers would string sand bags and fences along the dunes for the same purpose. Left undeveloped, the marsh would provide spectacular views. Generations of beach lovers could enjoy a protected retreat, right here in eastern North Carolina.

The ringing telephone dragged Connie from her thoughts. *Why doesn't Maggie answer that,* she wondered. *She must have stepped out.*

"Hello?" Connie said brusquely. She didn't like her thoughts interrupted.

A hoarse, familiar voice mocked her. "Foxed you again, didn't I, Missy? You'll never get approval for Turtle Nest. That's what you get for lying." The old senator's voice was raspy with age and cigar smoke.

Connie slammed the phone back on its cradle as if it were Clarence Roberts' face. *Old buzzard.* She hoped he lived long enough to see himself outfoxed.

Instantly, her mind was made up. This party could make or break her company, but she would go down fighting. Her guests must incur no expense—even for hotel rooms. The politicians stayed too leery of their constituents to spend government money on a venture advertised as pleasurable.

Connie plopped into her chair and considered her options. There was $30,000 in the business account, plus another $2,000 in private funds. She could even sell Aunt Eleanor's jewels. She opened her wallet—$30 in bills. In frustration, she snapped two credit cards onto her desk. She was prepared to max these out, if need be.

She decided to present Lucy's idea of a party at Monday morning's staff meeting. She took out a pad and pencil and began preliminary planning. The idea could not be introduced without basic guidelines.

They would treat each legislator as a prime buyer—wine, dine, and coddle them into a generous mood. Transportation posed no problem. For a reasonable fee, Captain Bob would press the ancient *Wisteria* into service and ferry everyone to the island. Once there, the guests would get a short sales pitch and lots of good liquor and food.

She'd call it a beach party. Perhaps she would also invite influential investors and friends—to help twist reluctant political arms. The idea required ingenious planning, but was possible.

Satisfied that she was ready to face her staff, Connie shoved the credit cards back in her wallet and stood up. For over thirty years she'd avoided Roberts and been his victim. That was over. She'd face him head-on, and this time, she didn't intend to lose.

Chapter 2

▼

Home Fires

Connie drove to her small cottage on the inland waterway. Her view of the landscape spread over marsh grass, oyster beds, and brackish water. She preferred it that way. The sea was too noisy, too chaotic. Sure, she loved the ocean. But for daily living she preferred the order and solitude of the marsh.

At least, she once felt that way. Her home, like her business, burdened her. It had become a responsibility—another matter demanding her attention. Connie wondered why she remained tired and yes, depressed. Nowadays, everything turned into a chore. What gave her pleasure in the past required more energy than she could muster. She supposed she should go to her doctor for a physical. Maybe he would prescribe some pep pills for her.

Because of possible flooding from hurricanes, Connie's house was built on pilings. The space underneath served as her garage. Parking her car carefully between the posts, she walked up the stone steps to her front door. When she entered, Katie, her cat, scooted across the floor. Katie was the black and white stray who had claimed her. Captain Bob said she'd hung around the docks for weeks, existing off fish scraps and handouts. Starved and bedraggled, she appeared the loser of several squabbles with other animals. As Connie bought flounder, the cat had spotted her. Animals usually avoided Connie. Some sense told them they would not like her.

But not Katie. She rubbed against Connie's legs, only to be shooed away. After driving the two blocks to her home, Connie found the cat perched on her doorstep. Three times she took the animal back to the docks. Three times it followed her home. She considered taking it to the animal control shelter but didn't quite have the heart for that.

So the cat stayed. "If you're living here, you need a name," Connie had told her. "How about Betsy. When I was a child, we had a cat named Betsy." Connie never grew tired of watching the cat communicate her feelings. When she became aloof and standoffish, you sensed her displeasure in her face. When pleased, she became a different animal. Her tail flicked and she smiled. No one believed Connie's cat smiled, until they saw it.

Connie tried several names before she hit on Katie. "I once had an aunt named Kate. She reminded me of you—gave herself airs and acted special even though she was dirt poor. Do you like 'Katie'?" Instantly, the tail arched and flicked while black lips curved into a feline grin.

At first Katie lived outside. But every time the door cracked, she would slip in. Connie gave up. Now the cat spent her days curled in the sun by the bay window overlooking the Intracoastal Waterway. When Connie worked, Katie sat on her shoulder and flicked her tail across the page. If scolded, she turned her back and pouted until offered a Kitty Treat.

After deciding to keep the cat, Connie took her to the local veterinarian. For $100 she learned the animal was three years old, had worms, fleas, and a bad tooth. For $150 more, the worms and fleas were eliminated, the tooth pulled, and she was spayed. Katie sulked for a week, blaming Connie for her misfortune. Connie wondered if she would have stayed, had she known all that would befall her.

Katie became a healthy, beautiful cat. With one eye patched with black fur and the other entirely white, she looked like two different animals, depending on which side you saw. Spotted all over, the vet called her the Dalmatian cat. This did not make Katie smile.

Katie twined between Connie's legs in welcome. "Looks like it's you and me this weekend, Sweetie." Tomorrow night she was hosting a small dinner party for prospective clients. Other than that, she planned little but relaxing and forgetting Clarence Roberts.

"Miss Edmonds, is that you?" Dilcey Reynolds, Connie's cleaning lady, called from the kitchen. Dilcey entered the foyer, wiping her hands on a dishtowel. "I hope your party goes well tomorrow night, Miss Edmonds. I cleaned extra hard so everything would look nice."

"Thank you, Dilcey. It shows."

"Then I'll be getting my things and catching the four o'clock." Dilcey retreated to the kitchen and began collecting the innumerable shopping bags she always carried. With eight children, she depended on the generosity of others. Connie's neighbors brought Dilcey hand-me-down clothes; the butcher gave her extra soup bones. Dilcey was grateful for any handout.

In spite of her hard life, Dilcey seemed happy. *Not happy,* thought Connie. *Peaceful. Dilcey makes me feel peaceful.* With a start, Connie realized her spirits lifted in her maid's presence. How could that be? She knew little about Dilcey except that she supported her children with no help from a man. And she worked six days a week, cleaning for people in Southport. After a day's work, she took laundry home and ironed for some of her customers. Surely that kind of life could not bring peace.

Connie understood that Dilcey drew strength from her belief in God. She was one of the few people Connie knew who practiced their religion all week long. If Connie was home while Dilcey cleaned, she could hear her maid singing Gospel hymns. *Rock of Ages* or *Washed in the Blood of the Lamb* triumphed over the noisy vacuum cleaner. Connie admitted to herself that she enjoyed hearing Dilcey give voice to the lovely old melodies.

Dilcey spent Sundays at her church, all day Sunday. Connie learned that when she asked Dilcey to help her serve a Sunday brunch. Dilcey would never correct her employer, but Connie realized then that Dilcey disapproved of a party given on Sunday. Especially since she was serving Mimosas—those delicious concoctions of champagne and orange juice that add spice to any brunch.

"See you next week, Miss Edmonds. I've got to get home. I like to be there when my boy Ben gets off the bus. He's my one young'un who needs a little extra time with his Mama." Ready to go, Dilcey adjusted the violets pinned to her bodice and reached for her hat. Connie wondered why Dilcey took such pains with her dress. She had noticed that Dilcey always wore faded silk violets—artificial purple things with faux pearl centers. The tired little flowers mirrored Dilcey's own tired face.

As Dilcey adjusted the hat on her tight, salt-and-pepper curls, Connie could hold her tongue no longer. "For heaven's sake, Dilcey. You're just walking three blocks to the bus stop. Why are you putting on your hat?"

Dilcey turned her lovely smile on Connie. "Oh I believe the Lord wants us to look good all the time. Today He wanted me here cleaning your house. I've got to look my best when I'm doing the Lord's work. Bye, now."

After Dilcey left, Connie scooped up her cat and wandered into her great room. She wished she could share Dilcey's peace and love of her work. Mentally, she contrasted Dilcey's happiness with her own. *How could someone as poor as Dilcey find serenity while she, Connie, was so bored with life? Where did you find such joy?*

Cradling Katie, she kicked off her shoes and settled into a swinging papasan chair. Absentmindedly, she looked at her surroundings. She'd furnished her home with local antiques, crafts, and nautical curiosities. When Connie bought her house, it was little more than a shack. The location sold her. Nestled above the salt marsh, she enjoyed a view of the inland waterway and ocean beyond. She fished, crabbed, and harvested oysters in fertile offshore beds. A small dory was moored at the dock for that purpose.

The focal point of the great room, a concave bay window, framed her deck and the water. As Connie looked out, a huge yacht floated by, headed south down the Inland Waterway. She wondered about the people on board. Were they Northerners headed to Florida? Were they locals out for an afternoon cruise?

Beyond the living and dining area, two bedrooms completed the downstairs level. The second floor consisted of a spacious widow's walk. Legend held that women once scanned the sea from this vantage point, searching for husbands and lovers. Connie had glassed in the walk and now used it for her office. On the ground floor, the laundry room and garage shared space.

Horrified, her mother had protested. At seventy-five, Helen Edmonds retained her taste for the flamboyant and the expensive. "It's so ... so rustic. Why don't you build yourself a new house? You can certainly afford it!"

Connie laughed. "Let me fix it up, Mom. It'll be great." And it had been great—a haven—until recently. Now it felt more like a prison.

When Connie finished the renovations, her mother changed her opinion. "Perfect. Sophisticated, yet cozy."

Helen spent several weeks with her daughter throughout the year, shopping or relaxing in the sun. Connie's mother remained attractive and vivacious, with the energy of a forty-year-old. Her father continued working around the house and yard, but didn't try to keep up with his wife.

Katie slept in her lap. Absent-mindedly stroking her fur, Connie planned tomorrow night's dinner party. Cooking, like everything else, had become drudgery. Why spend her weekend in the kitchen just to please rich clients? Yet she couldn't ignore her business. Besides, she had shrimp in her freezer that she needed to use before the new season began.

Connie would season the shrimp then grill them beside ears of fresh corn. With a salad and sliced peaches, her meal would be complete. Light and summery, the dinner took little planning or effort. The men would expect dessert, though the women were probably dieting. She supposed she could fix something chocolate. Chocolate was always popular.

She had invited Tom Crouton from her staff and two couples who had shown interest in buying sizeable parcels of oceanfront real estate. Tom would flatter the wives and feign interest in the jaded opinions of the husbands. Rumor often linked Tom and Connie romantically, but that would never be. Muscular and handsome, Tom charmed everyone. A string of women vied for his attention. But he and Connie invested too much time and energy in their jobs for an affair. Besides, Connie had no interest in a man fourteen years her junior—even if his ice blue eyes did search your soul.

Connie hoped Tom would arrive early so they could discuss the party on Turtle Nest. She wanted him briefed before Monday's sales meeting. After considering the idea over the weekend, he could offer valuable ideas to her associates. She reached for her new trimline telephone to call and suggest he come at five o'clock for a drink and planning session. *Dang,* she thought as she dialed the number. *Will I ever get used to these push buttons? I miss the whirrs and clicks of my faithful old rotary phone."* A female voice answered, purring that Tom was in the shower. Connie left the message, but questioned its delivery. "Bimbo," Connie breathed, replacing the receiver.

The next evening, however, Tom arrived before the party started. He agreed with Lucy. A party on the island captured his imagination. Like the rest of Connie's staff, he'd suffered bitter disappointment at the news of probable defeat for the Turtle Nest development.

Her dinner party began smoothly. The clients, two wealthy New York couples who sailed to Florida every winter, complimented her food. "What is this bread, Connie? I've never eaten anything like it. Very tasty."

"They're called hushpuppies, Seth. We eat them with seafood and barbecue. Old salts standing around campfires first made them—to keep the dogs quiet. They cooked up a batch and threw them to the hounds shouting, 'Hush, puppy.'"

As they ate, conversation flowed, relaxed and jovial, until she served coffee. The couples expressed interest in properties selling for over a million dollars. Then Horace Ketchum suddenly turned on Connie. "What's this I hear about your involvement in the Belcher deal, Connie?"

Connie swallowed hard. The Belcher affair had taken place in Wilmington the year before. John Belcher promised investors huge returns, then siphoned the money into his own account. Realizing he could not keep ahead of the game, he fled the country, leaving debts, bad credit, families and retirees with depleted savings. Originally, Connie invested heavily with him, believing him an honest businessman. She had liquidated her holdings, though, when she sensed risky business.

"I invested with John Belcher early on, Horace. So did many people in Southport. But I pulled out when I learned his true nature." Long before others realized it, her keen business sense told her Belcher would go broke in the end.

Horace Ketchum raised an eyebrow and gave Connie a knowing smile, but said no more. The guests stayed another half an hour, but Connie sensed a change in atmosphere. The women appeared bewildered, the men recalcitrant. After telling them goodbye, she and Tom wondered about the implications of the evening.

On Monday, Connie learned the outcome of her dinner party. Horace Ketchum's secretary called at 9:00 A.M.

"Mr. Ketchum will not be investing with you, Miss Edmonds. He's heard from certain political sources that you became one of Mr. Belcher's biggest backers. He doesn't feel that he can do business with you if there's a blot on your reputation."

Damn, thought Connie. *Clarence Roberts again.* "Would Mr. Ketchum care to name the political sources, so I can defend myself?" she probed.

"That's all he told me, Miss Edmonds. Mr. Ketchum left for Europe this morning and does not want to discuss the matter further." The line went dead before Connie could answer.

Lowlife, thought Connie. *Doesn't even have the decency to call me himself.* She fumed for another hour as she prepared for her ten o'clock staff meeting.

Connie's coworkers were enthusiastic about Lucy's idea. A party on Turtle Nest might win approval for its development. In addition to her secretary Maggie and Tom Crouton, her three sales associates attended the meeting. These associates, two men and a woman, received a base salary and also worked on commission. Excellent at their jobs, they got big paychecks for their hard work. They realized if Turtle Nest materialized, they would never again have to stump for business.

Tom took over when Connie finished. "If we can interest enough legislators, maybe we can push Turtle Nest through sooner than expected. They might meet in special session. At least we could move forward in preliminary development if we have promises of enough 'yes' votes."

After the meeting, Tom cornered Connie. "Let's squelch Roberts once and for all. You know Roberts is behind that phone call from Horace Ketchum's secretary, backing out of his deal. We have no choice. You've built this company in spite of him. But you'll never pull off something as big as Turtle Nest with Roberts in the background."

"But how, Tom? You know we've tried before, but with no luck."

"Let me dig deeper into his background. We've never done more than scratch the surface. I can ask questions and find information unavailable to you. Being head of this company, *and* a woman, some people won't talk to you."

"Aggh," Connie fumed. "That woman thing again. Why should that hamper me?"

Tom laughed. "Oh, I've seen it help you, Miss Connie. You had old bald Herb Jones eating out of your hand last year—begging for help in signing away his millions."

"After I found his bifocals." Connie laughed. "See what you find, Tom. I'd gladly drag Roberts' name through dirt, even though he is in his eighties." Connie's mood altered. Somewhere, deep in her soul, the devil of revenge leered with satisfaction.

Chapter 3

New Challenges

Connie's first appointment after the sales meeting unsettled her routine. Father Robin Benson of St. Bettina's Church entered her office with hat in hand. She raised her eyes to a tall, thin man silhouetted in the doorway. Handsome in a craggy sort of way, he entered, hesitant and ill at ease. *He looks like Abraham Lincoln* she thought, *without the beard.* Like Lincoln, his limbs hung loosely and appeared unconnected to the rest of his body.

"Excuse me for interrupting, Miss Edmonds. But thank you for your generous donation to St. Bettina's. Lucy James telephoned me over the weekend."

Connie crossed the room with outstretched hand. She didn't relish the thought of dealing with a priest this morning. Still, she'd learned long ago that a few minutes of goodwill went a long way—especially with the clergy.

"Come in, Father Benson. Come in. And thank you for coming. It wasn't necessary. Lucy is a dear and old friend. I'm sure she told you. She is so excited about the church. She can be very persuasive about her projects.

"Please call me Robin, Miss Edmonds, or Father Robin as some of my parishioners prefer. Just not Father Robin Hood which the Sunday schoolers seem to think is hilariously funny."

Connie smiled. "Then I'll ask you to call me Connie. Please sit down. Tell me your plans. Lucy outlined only the basics." Maybe if she humored him for a few minutes, he would leave.

To her surprise, an immediate metamorphosis changed Robin Benson from a docile, languid priest to a fire-and-brimstone advocate. He took a chair and leaned forward. His large hands filled the air as he described restoration, redesign, and redecoration. The voice, though, was what seized your attention and held you captive. Rich and mellow, it rose and fell in crescendos that reached out, encircled, then carried you in an ever-widening tide until you grasped the expanse of his point of view.

"St. Bettina's is ancient, Miss Edmonds—Connie. The original structure was burned in 1776, torched by British forces during the Revolution. In 1843, the present church was erected where it now stands. During the War Between the States, Union forces used St. Bettina's as a hospital. After the hospital closed, legend has it that Yankee soldiers stabled their horses in the building. Then it became a school for Negro children.

"Upon entering the sanctuary, you see all the flags that ever flew over St. Bettina's—English, Spanish, the Betsy Ross flag of the Colonies, Confederate, Union, United States, and the North Carolina flag.

"Time and storms have inflicted structural damage on the old building, but never toppled it. With limited funds, vestries of the past one hundred years have patched and mended. Now the old church needs major overhaul. Support beams have rotted and one side of the building tilts as its foundation has sunk into the sandy soil.

"After needed structural work, the interior will be refurbished, the stained-glass windows cleaned and releaded. While not enlarging the sanctuary, plans call for rearranging the altar and pews for better use of space. Already ladies of the congregation are designing needlepoint prayer cushions and wall hangings celebrating two hundred years of God's providence for the old church.

"You must forgive me," Father Benson apologized when Connie put her hand to her temple. "I was a student of architecture before I went to seminary. And I love church history. This project consumes my interest. Please excuse me if I've bored you."

"On the contrary. You've brought the project to life. I just can't process all that information in a few minutes. But I do admire your passion."

Father Benson leaned back in his chair and rubbed his forehead, gathering strength to broach the true reason for his visit. "Lucy serves on our board of directors. She and I hope that you will too. You would enjoy being with her. And quite frankly, we could not afford your business acumen otherwise. You know more about construction than any of us. Having your name on our board offers free advertisement for your company and this will be a statewide project. St. Bettina's belongs to all of North Carolina. We solicit funds from numerous sources. Your name, and that of your company, would embellish our letterhead." Long ago Father Benson had learned to appeal to the secular as well as the spiritual.

Connie stared at the clergyman, then swallowed hard to hide her irritation. How dare this man she'd never met come into her office and unload his burdens? She had plenty of work to do without getting involved with some church. Lucy James probably put him up to this—more of her plans to straighten out Connie's life. Still, he was a priest. She couldn't lose her temper with a priest, could she?

"Oh. I don't know Father," Connie murmured with fake civility. "I suppose Lucy told you I don't get involved in church work. And I stay pretty busy."

Relenting at present, the priest unfolded his lanky frame from the chair and walked toward the door. "Please think about it, he said. "We do need you."

Father Benson left quickly, showing himself out.

"Of course you'll do it, Connie," Tom Crouton said when she told him. "Think of the free advertising. And it's so—so legitimate. Clarence Roberts can't throw dirt on this."

Connie admitted that Tom had some good points. She made her decision to join the board from a business standpoint rather than a personal one. The name Connie Edmonds—Edmonds Real Estate and Development Company—was added to those of other supporters and board members on the St. Bettina's Episcopal Church Restoration Project. But she was still irritated with Lucy for interfering in her personal life.

Lucy phoned later in the week. Excitement bubbled over in her voice. "I'm thrilled you're on the board, Con. All the more reason for us to stay in touch. I'll be in Southport on Thursday for the first directors' meeting. Let's eat an early dinner before the meeting."

Connie sighed. Lucy was so exuberant. She never could stay mad at her. "Come by my place then, she said. "I'll fix us a light supper. You've never seen my home or met Katie." Connie knew Lucy had moved into an expensive townhouse when she married wealthy Charlie James. She hoped her friend would approve of her modest home. Thank goodness Dilcey had cleaned the day before. Without Dilcey, her cottage would revert to chaos.

But Lucy effused when she saw the bungalow. "It's so you, Connie. Understated, but elegant. Charlie and I plan on building a beach house at Morehead next year. Maybe you can help."

"Always happy for the business." She showed her friend the rest of the cottage. Katie took an instant liking to Lucy and helped conduct the tour perched on her slender shoulder.

Connie served their meal on the deck overlooking the Intracoastal Waterway. At low tide a pungent, salty smell saturated the marsh. Creatures, hidden when water flooded the salt grass, scurried about doing their chores. A young boy waved to them from his jon boat. At intervals he stood in the small craft, throwing his cast net in a wide arc, then slowly drawing it back to him. From their perch on Connie's deck, they saw the boy catch bait, small fish, even an occasional crab.

They dined on cold crab and white wine. Lucy entertained Connie with stories about fellow board members. With her quick wit and lively imagination, she summed up each personality.

"Of course there's you and me. It's obvious why they asked you. I was chosen because Charlie is rich. He'll donate lots of money to the project." Lucy, as usual, spoke her thoughts."Then there's the bishop. Burly Peters. He's originally from Wilmington. He's the spiritual leader for all the Episcopal churches in eastern North Carolina. That's over one hundred churches, if you count mission parishes. It's an honor, but a huge responsibility for one so young. Burly's a doll. His name suits him perfectly. He's a big, burly, teddy bear of a man. One of the kindest souls you'll ever meet. Joshua Dunn is from Asheville. Father Robin invited board members from around the state and Dunn represents western North Carolina. I don't have a feel for him yet, though he seems rather cold and distant. He developed those condos at the ski resorts around Beech Mountain and Boone. Maybe you two will find common ground, with your real estate interests. Besides Father Benson, other members include Mrs. Pauline DuVall and her husband Sims. Sims is a hardware salesman. That's all I know about him. His wife overshadows him. He's a non-person, really. Pauline is a matriarch, self-appointed historian, and snob. She always puts on airs, which is ridiculous because Sims' family has the money. But you'd never know that, listening to Pauline."

Later, when Connie met her fellow board members, she found Lucy's observations to be accurate. She liked Burly Peters at once. Usually she avoided religious men, but Burly exuded warmth and good humor. She felt comfortable in his presence. Except for the clerical collar, he looked like the stevedores she saw unloading cargo ships in Wilmington. Lucy failed to mention Bishop Peters was black. She probably hadn't noticed. But this was 1977, in eastern North Carolina, so it was noteworthy. Connie wondered if integrating the board was another attempt at reaching all segments of society—for support and fundraising. No harm in that.

Joshua Dunn was enigmatic. Ruggedly handsome, cold, austere and aloof, he socialized little. Connie supposed they shared similar business interests, but didn't make the effort to find out. She preferred hearing Burly's anecdotes of Sunday school antics in his former parish.

Heavily made up, heavyset, doused in heavy perfume—Orange Blossom, probably—Pauline DuVall descended on Connie. Large fake pearls wriggled in rolls of fat around her neck. Her hair flamed orange. Connie couldn't believe it. She looked again. Brassy orange, brushed high from her forehead, Pauline's hair crowned her head like an out-of-control bird nest. Listless as foam from a rolling ship, a pale, mousy man trailed in her wake. Sims DuVall, she assumed. Pauline's enormous red lips bellowed. "My dear, is your family from Onslow County? The Edmonds who own the large horse farm on highway 17?"

"No ma'am. My father works for the railroad. The rest of my family raises hogs in Edgecombe County. They're pig farmers, Mrs. DuVall."

"Hmmph!" Mrs. DuVall voiced her displeasure and huffed off to the coffee and dessert table. Sims smiled wanly, then followed his wife.

Father Benson called for order, but made it clear he did not direct the committee. Electing a chairperson became the first order of business.

Bishop Peters declined immediately, citing conflict of church duties. He suggested a local chairperson so decisions and problems could be dealt with first hand. Only Connie and Mr. and Mrs. DuVall lived in the area. Connie pleaded business pressures as reason for not choosing her. Pauline practically climbed on the table, begging the board for the position. No one seriously considered Sims.

Before the vote, Lucy cornered Connie at the water fountain. "Please, Con. Be our chairperson. I realize you're busy, but can you imagine Pauline at the helm? She'd make our lives miserable. She'd probably want her portrait hung in the nave of the restored church. We can't inflict that on future generations."

Connie had not intended on becoming involved in affairs outside her business. Still, Lucy had a point. Life with Pauline as chair would be hell. She decided to vote for herself and accept the chairmanship if elected.

The tally showed four votes for Connie, three for Pauline. Connie knew where two of Pauline's votes came from. Searching the faces of other committee members, she wondered who cast the third vote. Would this cause problems in the future?

She thanked the members for their faith in her. Pauline fumed in her chair, mumbling something about "pigs in high places." Connie could almost see steam rising from the orange hair. She thought she saw a smile flicker across Sims' pale lips. When she looked again, it had vanished.

Father Benson suggested they begin soliciting estimates for renovation. Connie knew she would waste valuable time if she had to be on site with contractors. Remembering the priest's background in architecture and his obvious enthusiasm for the project, she appointed Robin Benson her assistant. Robin seemed pleased with the duty—as long as he didn't shoulder full responsibility. Pauline continued to fume. Now she mumbled that she knew a great deal about church architecture.

The session adjourned with a decision to meet monthly. Father Benson promised reports from several contractors for the next meeting. As they left, Lucy twined her arm around Connie. "Father Robin's so handsome, Con—and a bachelor."

Connie smiled. "Luce, the first time I met you, thirty-two years ago, you tried luring me into chasing men. Do you think of nothing else?"

Lucy kissed her cheek and climbed into her silver Lincoln Continental. She gave her friend a secret smile, a wave, and drove off.

Chapter 4

▼

Amelia

She was late. Five, ten, fifteen minutes. As he waited, Tom Crouton studied the sentimental carvings on the table: hearts with "Jerri and Sam forever" and "Bill loves Frances" etched crudely into the dark wood. He fidgeted. Something about this smoky bar gave him the creeps.

Earlier in the week, he had entered Connie's office flaunting a thin file folder. "We're learning quite a bit about Senator Clarence Roberts. He's certainly the ladies' man—or was, in his prime."

"Oh, Tom. Everyone knows that. Including his wife."

"Yeah. But some of the ladies he squired around were involved in shady political deals."

Connie's interest piqued. "Oh? Tell me more."

"Actually, I only have suspicions right now. But I'm going to Raleigh on Thursday to meet Roberts' other daughter, Amelia."

"Other daughter?" Connie dropped in her chair as if she'd been punched in the stomach. "In all the years I've dealt with Roberts I've never heard of another daughter."

"Oh yes, there's another daughter. I found her through my expert sleuthing and superior detective skills. For some reason she hates Daddy and Daddy doesn't want anyone to know about her. She's anxious to help us destroy her father, and for that we're going to pay her a bundle.

"I'm hoping Amelia will let me in on family secrets. Roberts is far too crafty to leave a trail. But the old fox must have slipped somewhere. Give me a few weeks and I'll fill your pretty ears with lurid details."

"Okay, Sherlock." Connie couldn't help laughing at her cocky assistant. "Just try to go easy on your expense account."

Then she was there. Amelia finally deigned to show. She slid across the sticky vinyl seat, snuggling close to him, melding her middle-aged body into his young one. "Sorry I'm late. Traffic, you know. Bring me a Bloody Mary," she told the bartender who approached their table.

"Did you bring the information?" Tom asked. Now he saw the bar for what it was—a seedy hangout for has-beens, rather than a romantic hideaway. He wanted out. Especially since she was snuggling closer, resting her hand on the inside of his thigh.

"Don't be in such a hurry, Honey. I said I was sorry for being late. But the night's young. We've got lots of time." With one hand, the woman reached for a cigarette. With the other, she began stroking Tom's thigh, moving upward toward his crotch. Tom crossed his legs, turning away from her as he scrunched between the wall and the table.

"What's the matter, Babe? Afraid?" Amelia sat up, laughing bitterly. The laugh ripened into a prolonged, phlegmy cough, which tore from her chest like regurgitation, shaking her frame and leaving her weak.

"Sorry," she gasped after some moments. "I really should quit these things. Like father, like daughter, you know." Amelia wiped mucus from her mouth, examined the residue, then demurely tucked the Kleenex into her bodice. "Now what was it you wanted?"

Again her hand was on his thigh, stroking, edging upward. Tom choked out his next words, uncomfortable, but not about to leave. Amelia was his ace in the hole. "Your father, remember? You said you had information about your father."

"My father. The Honorable Senator Clarence Roberts. Not many people know I'm related to the old crook. I've gone to great lengths to hide that fact. So has he. You did some expert sleuthing to find me."

"My employer needs to know about your father. We'll pay you well for useful information."

Amelia laughed again. This time, without disastrous results. "I imagine your employer is Connie Edmonds. It could be any number of people, he's made so many enemies. But Connie is the only one he bothers with these days."

"Suppose Miss Edmonds *is* my employer? Why does your father hate her so? Oh, I know the story about your sister. But that was a long time ago. And it's not like Miss Edmonds murdered her. Amanda took her own life."

"You don't know my father very well. He has to blame someone for all his badness. He's blamed me for years—for lots of things. He blames Connie for Amanda's death. In his warped mind, Amanda was the one good thing in his life. Clarence Roberts has done so many rotten things over the years. Adultery, scandals, lies, probably even murder. But Amanda. He figured he'd be forgiven all his sins just because he fathered her. When she died, he lost his ticket to Heaven. That's what he blames Connie Edmonds for—eternal damnation. Don't get me wrong. I loved my sister. But my father made her into some sort of saint."

"Well that's all well and good," Tom said. "But I need hard information—facts. What kind of proof do you have of your father's crimes?"

"I've brought names—names of butlers, gardeners, maids. One of them will talk—for money, for revenge, for notoriety. You must understand. I was a child in that house. And I was sent to boarding school when I was only nine years old. It wasn't until I was an adult that I realized my family life was far from normal. But our help knew. They must have. They can give you specifics."

Amelia Roberts now had him pinned between herself and the wall. Tom knew he would run if she weren't such a valuable pawn.

"Okay. I'll pay for that information. But tell me more about your home life. I'm after dirt on your father. What did he blame you for? Why didn't he love you like he loved Amanda? Why are you even willing to rat on the old man?"

Tom watched as Amelia's flaccid, overly made-up lids narrowed to thin, lethal slits. He'd seen that look before. At the museum, at the reptile cage. He'd intuitively known the snake was filled with hate—hate for its cage, hate for its captors, hate for itself. Amelia's eyes mirrored that hate.

"Rat on my old man? You want to know about my childhood? Ha! I'll tell you about my childhood. There was no love there. Not for me, anyway. I was always the misfit—too big, too bony—not like pretty little Amanda. I could never please my father. I tried, at first. After a while I just gave up. Amanda pleased him just by being alive. I think he scorned the day he even sired me.

"My mother loved me. Without her, I would have gone crazy. She taught me everything I know about men. How to attract them, how to please. She was a showgirl before she married my father. He found her dancing in some little bar, trying to make it on Broadway. She taught me well." Amelia's fingers wandered again, this time with a definite target in mind.

"I remember my favorite times. My mother would take me into her dressing room after her bath and let me watch her dry herself. She showed me all her seductive moves. How to draw the towel in and out of the secret crevices of her body—between her legs, under her arms, across her breasts—using the towel like a sort of penis or stimulator to excite herself and the man watching her. It reminded me of the bow of a violin, drawn seductively over taut strings.

"Then she would reach for her powder puff and dust herself all over. Quick, staccato pats heightening the languid sensation of the towel into sharp, prickly pangs of desire. She dusted her whole body, beginning at her neck and working down to her feet using those same quick pats. Then she would return, giving her sensual parts extra attention—raising each breast, fondling each nipple—clouds of white powder bouncing into the air like some ethereal mist surrounding a modern day Aphrodite. She finished by giving her woman's place a final dusting, turning, bending, so that I had a perfect view of her dark jungle, lined pearly pink, opened, anxious, flecked with white powder like sugar on a delicious doughnut some man would love to eat.

"My father found us one day. He made something harmless and innocent into a terrible sin. 'What the hell are you doing?' he shouted. 'You're a pervert. A nasty little pervert!'

"He grabbed my shoulder and dragged me from the room. But not before I had my say. 'You're jealous, old man,' I shouted at him. 'You're jealous of me. Oh, I hear you at night when I listen at your bedroom door, begging, pleading. 'Come on, honey, hold it, stroke it. Maybe I can get it up if you'll help me.' You're jealous because she doesn't want you anymore. She'd rather spend her time with me.'

"He hit me then, sending me sprawling across the room into the wall. I was unconscious for hours. When I was well enough, I was sent away to boarding school. So I hate him. After that day, I made up mind to hate him forever. And I have. Right now, I'm just waiting for him to die. My mother tricked him into setting up an irrevocable trust in my name. When he dies, I'll be moderately wealthy. In the meantime, I'll hurt him any way that I can. So here's your list. Did you bring the money?"

Tom took the crumpled sheet of paper from Amelia, read it, handed her a thousand dollars. She tucked the money into her bodice next to the filthy handkerchief. Tweaking his penis and kissing him soundly on the lips, she rose to go. "I can see you're not out for any fun tonight. Too bad. Feels like a pretty good-sized dick between your legs. Think I'll find me someone more willing, now that I've got some cash."

Tom watched the old slut waggle over to the bar, teetering on a pair of run-down high heels. Sliding her gawky frame between two cowboy types, she reached for her new-found money. "What a pitiful woman," Tom whispered to the bartender who came to wipe the table.

The man shot him a quizzical look, then began laughing. "Woman? Woman! You thought that was a woman? What an idiot! The biggest queer in a joint full of queers just goosed you. Bet that's a first for you, pretty boy!"

The barkeep had more to say. Tom never heard him. Suddenly he realized the room was full of men, only men, some beautiful enough to model in magazines. Even this impression was short-lived. The bile in his stomach churned and spewed, gurgling to the surface, sending him to the john, his hand covering his mouth.

Chapter 5

Two Visitors

Maggie had sent out invitations for the party at Turtle Nest. The festivities would occur on the Fourth of July weekend. Each year, Southport hosted an Independence Day celebration. This began as a small event, but grew yearly. Visitors from across the state flocked to the little town. The legislators would enjoy coveted political exposure. What better campaign strategy than attendance at a memorial honoring the founding of our nation, then working for your constituents by fact-finding on a barrier island?

"I've heard from thirty representatives and twenty senators, Connie, plus four of your friends. So far we've only received two negative responses. Looks like the party will be a complete success."

Connie made a face. "What politician wouldn't spend a holiday on a resort island—while getting his picture in the paper? Will most of them bring their wives?"

"Yes. In fact, I'm sure the wives are encouraging their husbands to attend."

"Oh well. I suppose there's no backing out now. The party will be a reality. Janie will oversee the event. You'll work closely with her. In fact, let me have the list of acceptances. I'll begin discussing them with her right away."

Connie entered Janie Kilpatrick's office and found the tall blonde pouring over lists of caterers. Janie was a sales associate and a smart businesswoman. She shouldered the added duties of the party with vivaciousness and charm.

"Con," Janie said, "I think I've found the perfect caterer, and she's right here in Southport—a bakery named Betty Sue's Sugar Cube. I know, sounds like sticky éclairs and too many calories. But Betty Sue caters on the side. She's a gourmet cook. Plus, I like patronizing local folks whenever possible. It's good for our business.

"I thought we'd prepare a shrimp fest. That's really the only choice on the island. We'll grill chicken for those who don't want seafood. But mostly we'll serve shrimp. Betty Sue knows wonderful recipes for grilled shrimp, shrimp and grits, shrimp Creole—the works."

"Good grief, Janie. How much will this cost?" Connie rolled her eyes in horror.

"A pittance, compared to your profits if you develop Turtle Nest. Now go do something useful. I'm planning a party. And it's only six weeks away." Janie gently shoved her boss toward the door.

"Insubordination," Connie murmured, knowing Janie was not at all insubordinate. She hired only the best, paid excellent wages, and received quality work in return.

She wished she could summon excitement for the party, though. In years past, she would have happily hosted a party that would be the talk of North Carolina—and be covered in society columns throughout the state. Now it seemed another chore added to her over-burdened shoulders.

When Connie got home her answering machine light was flashing twice. She hoped the messages were salespeople who had hung up.

Father Benson's voice sounded when she pushed the message button. "Connie, could I meet you around lunchtime tomorrow? I need your advice on some early construction bids. I'll only take a few minutes."

The second caller was her mother. "Connie, dear. I'm coming to Wilmington tomorrow. Thought I'd ride down and let you take me to lunch. I'm spending the afternoon poking through antique shops. If you're sweet, I may spend the night."

Dang, Connie thought. She kept her mother out of her business and personal life whenever possible. Helen flaunted her stubbornness and firm opinions. Well, she couldn't do anything about it. Father Benson and her mother would arrive at the same time.

The next day, Father Benson proved anxious to begin the renovation. He had obtained three initial estimates for structural repair. Two contractors suggested using new timbers for stabilization of the sunken foundation. The third planned on jacking up the building and replacing support structures as needed. Of course, his bid exceeded their budget.

"I suppose we should let the board make this decision," Connie mused. "But if we're hoping this renovation will last another two hundred years, we must replace everything that's rotted. I say let's continue talking to the builder who suggests doing the more thorough job."

"I agree, Connie. Just wanted your okay. I'll call the bishop and Lucy and ask their opinion. If they agree, that would give us a majority decision."

"Oh darling. Maggie didn't tell me you had a handsome gentleman with you." Among other things, Helen Edmonds was an ostentatious flirt. Maggie stood helplessly by the door as a tiny, red-suited whirlwind breezed into the office.

Connie grimaced. "Father Benson, this is my mother, Helen Edmonds. She knows no shame or manners."

As Father Benson stood, then stooped and extended his hand, Connie imagined a tall bird bending to scrutinize a ladybug. "Hello, Mrs. Edmonds. I hope you'll call me Robin. I'm the priest at St. Bettina's Episcopal Church. Did Connie tell you she's helping with our renovation project?"

"No," Helen pouted. "Connie never tells me anything about her life."

Connie smothered her annoyance and kissed her mother. "Mom's in town shopping for antiques—and applying her monthly dose of mother-daughter guilt."

Father Benson smiled. "Antiques. My first love. After the church, of course." He and Helen began chatting about favorite periods of furniture and savvy purchases. Connie realized if she hoped to work that afternoon, she should feed them, then send them off to the shops together.

They lunched at the Crab's Claw, a small shack perched at the end of the community pier. Not known for fancy décor or posh service, it catered to local patrons. Caught that morning in water less than a hundred yards from the cooking pot, the crabs oozed a sweet, brackish flavor. They were served one of two ways—steamed or deviled. Father Benson and Connie chose steamed, preferring their crabmeat unadulterated by spices or breading. "Too much work," proclaimed Helen, choosing the deviled version. "I like my crab picked out and edible."

Helen monopolized the conversation. "Robin's extending his lunch hour and taking me to several shops off the tourist path. I need a small chest for the foyer—mahogany, I think. I want visitors to see my beautiful antiques as soon as they enter my house. I can find my way home when we're through."

Annoyed that her mother was using the priest's first name, Connie realized she still felt uncomfortable calling him Robin. She left the shoppers abruptly. "All right, Mom. I'll be home around six."

For two hours the antiquers examined, hunted, and bargained. Helen found a mahogany chest that she loved, but the top drawer sat ajar and would not close.

She scratched her nose and considered the dilemma. "I don't know, Robin. This is a fine piece. But I did plan on finding something I could use right away."

"I believe you should buy what you love." The priest caressed the fine wood. "One of my parishioners, Jim Cooper, is an expert craftsman. He restores furniture for the museum in Raleigh. Jim's going to do some interior work for us at the church, when we get that far along. If I ask him, he'll fix the drawer. But I warn you, he stays busy. And his craft is not one you hurry. It will be a while before you get the chest, but you'll be satisfied with the results."

Helen bought the chest and resigned herself to keeping the plant stand in her foyer a while longer.

Chapter 6

Progress and Questions

At the next board meeting of the St. Bettina's restoration project, Pauline DuVall raged at Connie. "You mean you made a major decision regarding the church foundation without contacting the whole board? So what if you had a majority. You needed everyone's input. My cousin Hiram up in Columbus County knows something about building. He'd advise us—free of charge."

Connie pictured a male version of Pauline named Hiram. "No thanks," she muttered.

Father Benson rose to Connie's defense. "Pauline," he fumed, "don't take your anger out on Miss Edmonds. Blame me if you want. I made the original suggestion."

"Okay, I will blame you," shouted Pauline. "You and your group of cronies are determined to control this committee."

Father Benson's face became livid red, then stark white. "Pauline, you are nothing but trouble. You are just jealous because...."

Bishop Peters stood and placed his arm around the errant priest. "Sit down, Robin," he murmured. "Sit down and cool off."

As Bishop Peters led the angry man to his chair, Connie studied the others. Sims DuVall and Joshua Dunn stared at the floor. Pauline gloated with hurt pride and righteous indignation. Lucy glared at Pauline as if she would gladly pull the few remaining orange strands from her head.

Connie summoned her courage. "Pauline." She refused the woman any advantage of formality. "You're right. We should involve the board on major decisions. But we must proceed as quickly as possible. With your known good taste and preference for quality, we naturally assumed you would want only the highest standards. Were we wrong?"

Connie watched as Pauline's expression changed from self-righteousness to bewilderment. "Well, no. No." The confused woman hesitated. "You're right. I do have extremely refined taste and settle for only the best. But—but we all need a voice in making decisions."

So that's how you handled Pauline—with flattery. Connie relaxed. "Father Benson serves as my building assistant. We must rely on him to assure valuable time is not wasted. We need your input on truly major projects." *Like installing the toilet,* thought Connie.

As Pauline relented, Joshua Dunn glared at Connie. "See that you do involve us in the future, Miss Edmonds." In her business, Connie frequently dealt with rich, vain women like Pauline. But something in Dunn's stare and tone of voice sent icicles shooting down her spine.

After a brief walk outside Father Benson returned to the meeting and spent the next hour describing plans for the restoration of the church. "It's going to be glorious, my friends—a structure worthy of our illustrious heritage and our great God. The roof will be entirely reshingled using English cedar shake shingles donated by a parishioner. The interior is slated for a complete overhaul. Jim Cooper, our master craftsman, will refinish the pews and altar. The stained-glass windows will be cleaned and releaded. Future generations will thank us for such quality restoration work."

This man has a true gift, thought Connie. *He becomes a different man when he talks about something he loves—compelling his listeners to visualize what he's talking about. I wish he could convey my vision of Turtle Nest to certain politicians.*

Connie's thoughts collided with a half-conceived plan that had already been residing in her brain. Of course! Why not suggest that Father Benson speak at the shrimperoo? Not on development at Turtle Nest, but about local history and the work at St. Bettina's. Captivated by his enthusiasm, legislators would return home and contact parishioners in support of the project. And she could advertise the fact that an expert on local church history would speak. The statesmen would be convinced that they were serving God and their country. By the time they left the island, after having eaten her shrimp and imbibed her liquor, supporting the development of Turtle Nest would become their civic duty.

"I don't know, Connie," Father Benson wavered when she cornered him after the meeting. "I can preach to my congregation—but not 200 politicians. What could I possibly say to interest them?"

"You have no choice. You'll have a captive audience, relaxed and in a festive mood. The added publicity would cost St. Bettina's thousands of dollars. Just say what you said tonight. You'll do fine."

"Well," Father Benson conceded, "I pressured you to join the board, using your business sense and experience as an argument. I just didn't know that business sense included me. But I have one condition. Quit calling me Father Benson. Even your mother calls me Robin."

Connie blushed. "You're right. It's time. I promise."

When Connie described Robin's role in the shrimp fest, Janie whooped with pleasure. "What an inspired idea. I've arranged the food and logistics—how we'll ferry people to the island, chairs, tables, that sort of thing. But I didn't know what they'd do once they landed."

"Transporting more than 200 people takes time. We can entertain our first guests with short trips around the island, light hors d'oeuvres, and weak drinks. I want them relaxed when we talk to them, but I want them sober," Connie said.

"We'll congregate around three o'clock for a short sales pitch—so subtle they won't know it's business. I won't speak, just mingle. You talk a few minutes—describe the day's festivities and our plans for the island. Be brief. I'm mailing each legislator an itinerary plus a glossy brochure on how the island will look when it's developed.

"Bill Pace of the North Carolina Wildlife Protection Agency will be our keynote speaker. Bill realizes that unless protected, the turtles will die out. He hates human encroachment in natural habitats, but knows it's inevitable. The next best thing, he believes, is educating people and getting them interested in wildlife protection. In the end, this may prove the wisest course. Informed citizens become advocates for all wildlife—especially the turtles.

"We'll end with Father Benson. He's not a fire-and-brimstone preacher, until he starts on local and church history. That helps us end on an upbeat note. Father Benson is a quiet, shy man. But when he speaks on one of his pet subjects, he changes. He relaxes, his eyes sparkle, his face glows. He becomes quite handsome, really."

"Goodness," Janie interrupted. "Father Benson has certainly made you a convert."

Connie started. It was true. She loved St. Bettina's—its beauty and its history. Still, the religious part offered no allure.

But was there more? Always brutally honest with herself, Connie wondered if she were attracted to Robin Benson? No man ever held her interest for long. Occasionally, she dated clients or businessmen from Wilmington. But soon they appeared concerned only with her money or their ego.

Robin was different. His quiet humor lifted the depression and exhaustion that plagued her. And his many hobbies and pursuits made him fascinating.

".... and I thought we'd run buses back and forth from the larger hotels in Wilmington," Janie said. "After the party, many of our guests won't be in any condition to drive. Our staff is coordinating reservations. I wish we could house them in Southport. But we don't have accommodations for that many people."

Connie dragged her thoughts back to Janie, realizing her mind had strayed far from the shrimperoo. "Sounds great. I'll work with Bill Pace and Father Benson on their talks and leave the rest to you. July Fourth will be here before we know it."

At home that evening, Connie put a Bee Gees disco album on her stereo, scooped up Katie, stretched out on a deck chair, and continued her thoughts from the morning. She'd worked hard the rest of the day, so had buried the nagging question of her feelings for Robin Benson. Now she would deal with it.

The sun had dipped behind the pines across the Waterway. Though out of sight, it left trees outlined in gold and shot rose-colored rays into the sky. The water and marsh grass darkened to ghostly gray. Two egrets, pecking for their last evening meal, glimmered starkly white in contrast.

Connie sighed. She loved it here. Though she'd lost interest in decorating and cleaning, her home remained her sanctuary. A place to retreat and shove the day's demons into a corner. In her business she traveled, but preferred her home to any motel or resort.

Now to the business of Robin. She would sort this mess out once and for all. Could she, at forty-nine, be falling for a man? And a priest at that. She didn't need involvement at this stage in her life. And he'd given no indication of any interest in her on a personal level. On the contrary, he acted shy and ill at ease in her presence.

Mentally, she evaluated him. He was certainly well educated—a fascinating conversationalist. But there was more. Robin had a gentleness, an assurance that held and protected you. Ridiculous. She'd taken care of herself all her life. Why did she suddenly feel she wanted more?

"Shit," Connie muttered, irritated at herself. She liked things black and white, yes or no.

The jangle of the telephone startled her. Surprisingly, Robin's voice sounded when she answered. "Connie, I need to talk to you. Could I come over?"

That was the last thing she wanted. But how do you tell a priest you couldn't see him because you're considering a relationship with him? "I'm really tired tonight, Robin," she hedged. "Come by the office next week."

"It concerns your mother's mahogany chest. Jim Cooper found something when he began repairing it. Something that could upset your mother."

In spite of herself, Connie was intrigued. What mystery hid in a mahogany chest? Curiosity won. "Come over then. If you think it's important."

He arrived in five minutes. Connie led him to the deck and handed him a glass of wine. Robin inhaled deeply. "As a priest, I believe God is everywhere. But I'm sure He makes His home in Southport—on the marsh."

Connie noticed how often Robin spoke of God as if He were present. That frightened her. It seemed unnatural. Changing the subject, she questioned the priest. "What did Cooper find in the chest? Did you bring it?"

Wordlessly, Robin handed her a manila folder. "Be careful. This is quite old."

Connie opened the folder and found a single sheet of paper, brown with age and crumbling at the edges. The writing on it was almost illegible in the dusk. She carried the folder to her desk, switched on the study light, and read:

I did it. God forgive me. I will burn in Hell.
Suzanne Cogdill Marshburn, May, 1859

Robin followed her into the room and stood over her shoulder. She inhaled his masculinity as she turned inquiring eyes toward him. This would never do. Concentrate on the question at hand.

"Cooper found this wedged in your mother's chest. We thought the drawer was broken. It was just jammed. The note dropped out when he removed the runner.

"My question is whether or not to tell your mother. I don't know who Suzanne Marshburn was or why she thought she'd go to Hell. But we can find out. This chest is a local piece. But maybe you'd rather not mention this. If you think she'll be upset, Jim will reattach the runner, destroy the note, and deliver the chest."

"Oh, no. This will fascinate her. We must find out about Suzanne Marshburn. Mother would be furious if we did otherwise." Connie realized she, too, was intrigued.

"I agree. Just wanted your approval. I'll contact Helen in the morning and see if she wants me to proceed with the investigation. In the meantime, Jim will put the chest back together."

"Knowing Mother, she'll want your assistance, but will come to Southport to supervise. I'm probably in for an extended stay."

"I can imagine two intelligent ladies would sometimes be at odds." Retrieving the folder, he walked toward the door. "Goodnight, then. I'll call your mother in the morning."

After Robin left, Connie succumbed to exhaustion. The emotional stress of the evening, coupled with the wine, took their toll. Turning off the lights, she headed to the bedroom, Katie close on her heels. As she nestled beneath her sheets, Katie settled onto the pillow. Her mother was horrified that Katie slept with her. "If you need company in bed, take a man. They're much more satisfying than a cat."

Connie's last conscious thoughts pertained to whether or not Robin Benson would satisfy in bed. She slept fitfully as the question tormented her. Around midnight she slipped into the nightmare. She'd seen the demon before, but tonight it was more vivid than ever. "You're not worthy of Robin," the evil spirit cackled. "You're not worthy of love from any man." The dream was filled with black fog, high-pitched ringing, and the incessant jangle of the copper necklace that hung from the fiend's neck. The spirit swooped back and forth, sometimes in a corner of the room, sometimes right over her face. But always the noise—the jangling, ringing, and screeching that came straight from the gates of Hell.

Connie awoke, realizing that she was screaming. She lay there letting the sweat on her forehead cool and the horrible images recede. But the questions remained. Who was this she-devil? It was certainly a woman. And why did she always come when Connie became interested in a man?

Chapter 7

▼

Fuel for the Fire

Two weeks later Tom Crouton entered Connie's office and laid a thick file on her desk. "Here it is. The complete report on Senator Clarence Roberts. Cost you a bundle, but I think you'll agree it was worth every penny. Read it at your leisure. In a nutshell, it labels Roberts an incurable philanderer. Everyone knew and indulged his wandering eye—including his wife.

"What they didn't comprehend were the political shockwaves of these affairs. He bedded women of power—wives of governors and United States senators, congresswomen, presidential aides. Evidently, he slept with the wife of a vice president.

"We dug deep, interviewing household help, hotel staff long since retired, retrieving old phone records. It's a masterpiece of investigative work. I wish I knew the old codger's secret. I've never enjoyed that kind of success with women."

"Tom, I'm sure it's interesting reading. Use it as the basis for a best-selling novel. But let's destroy Roberts. If this goes public, people will do what you're doing—chuckle and say 'Lively old coot, wasn't he?' I want to put nails in his coffin, as well as through his heart, then bury the bastard."

"That's the beauty of this report, Connie. It's detailed. Detailed. There's strong indication Roberts secured political favors by using his sexual prowess. A male prostitute, if you will. I've heard of women doing that, but never a man. An example might be a close call on a bill crucial to Roberts' constituents back home.

Roberts woos the congresswoman who chairs the committee and presto—the bill passes.

"You'll also find some juicy information about his home life. That meeting I had with Amelia in Raleigh? Quite a story there. That alone would ruin his reputation.

"There's also evidence Roberts eyed the young boys and practiced some strange sexual customs. That's possibly not true, but adds spice to the tale."

Connie leaped from her chair. "Wonderful, Tom. You've done it. Roberts will look like a philandering Benedict Arnold when we finish with him. Please thank everyone on our staff who worked with you and the outside investigative agencies. If this report covers all you say, bonuses are due. You've wrapped this up nicely." Connie sighed, "I only wish my home life ran as smoothly."

"Uh,oh. Mom still visiting?"

"She arrived the day after Father Benson called about the note. Been hot on the trail ever since. I don't publicize it too much. I'd just as soon the Southport press not know. Not much goes on in this little town. This would be a sensational story and my mother loves publicity. But the way she's flitting around, it's only a matter of time."

"Has she solved the mystery?" Tom had met Helen Edmonds, thought her charming, was glad she wasn't his mother.

"They identified Suzanne Marshburn. That was public record. Her husband owned a large rice plantation just north of here—Marshlands, I believe. Suzanne came from England in 1855 and married John Marshburn. She bore Marshburn three children before he suffered a heart attack—in May, 1859. Everyone assumed he died of natural causes. He had just whipped one of his slaves when he clutched his heart and fell over dead." Connie shuddered. "I'm glad those days are gone.

"After the Civil War, Suzanne took her children and left for England. The newspaper at the time featured a story about poor widow Marshburn returning with her orphaned children to her father's home. Marshlands fell into disrepair. There the trail stops."

"Why is your mother still here, if there's no mystery?" Tom asked.

"Oh, but there's the note. Suzanne believed she deserved penance in Hell. Did she poison Marshburn—make it look like a heart attack? Had she committed some other heinous crime for which she damned herself?"

"Will your mother discover if Marshburn died of unnatural causes?"

"She may never prove anything. But she's learning all she can. Right now she's investigating old methods of poisoning. She and the town librarian are on a first name basis. Once or twice a week she drives up to the library in Wilmington. She and Father Benson are visiting Nettie Mae this afternoon."

"That old voodoo queen down at the end of Birch Street?"

"The same. Mom's latest lead is old slave medicine and potions. She's certain Nettie Mae can help her. She was heading there by herself last night after dark. Robin and I insisted she wait until this morning. And take him along."

"How much longer will she stay?"

"Lord only knows." Connie unconsciously adopted one of Robin's religious maxims. "Until she solves the mystery or I kick her out. Whichever comes first."

"Better you than me. I've gotta go. I've got work to do. My boss is a real witch."

Tom turned to leave, then added as an afterthought, "What you do with this report is your decision. Everyone who worked on this investigation will forget anything we learned about Roberts. That really isn't a problem. I'm the only one who knows how it all fits together. You'll know too, once you read it. I'll disregard what I know, unless you ask for further assistance."

Connie held the document long after Tom left. *I've got him,* she mused. *Finally—I've caught the old rascal. After years of torment, I can silence him for good. We can embarrass him into never showing his face in public again.* She put the file with her purse. *I'll read every detail, then destroy the old coot.*

When Connie arrived home, her mother grabbed her by the arms and twirled her around the kitchen like a child on her birthday. Connie wanted nothing more than to kick off her shoes, relax, and begin reading the Roberts file. That wouldn't happen. "Nettie Mae had a gun, Connie. One of those old-fashioned, long-barreled squirrel guns. Shot right over our heads and said she didn't want white folks on her property. When Robin shouted to her, she raised her gun and hollered, 'This time I be shooting low.' So we turned and ran for the car." In her excitement Helen adopted Nettie Mae's dialect.

"Well I'm glad you're giving up. Sounds dangerous to me."

"Oh, I'm not giving up. Oh, no. Joe Johnston, one of Nettie Mae's great-grandchildren, keeps the yard and gardens at St. Bettina's. Robin's introducing me to him tomorrow. I'll have no trouble talking to him. You know how I love gardens. In fact, Robin's asked me to help redesign the church gardens, once the renovation is completed."

Connie groaned inwardly at the prospect of her mother extending her stay. "What about Dad? Doesn't he want you at home? He'd never forgive me if anything happened to you."

"Your father acts like he misses me, but I know he and Billy Lewis play poker every night."

Her mother returned to her story. "Let me tell you what else I learned about Suzanne Marshburn. After Nettie Mae chased us off her property, I spent the afternoon reading in the library. Suzanne came from a wealthy family herself."

"Well, that's understandable. John Marshburn would have wanted a cultured and refined wife to mother his children and grace his plantation."

"You're right, of course. Her family lived in Dover, England. On the seacoast. Suzanne's father was a merchant and sea captain named William Cogdill. She was the only girl in a family of six—four boys, Suzanne and her father. Mrs. Cogdill died when Suzanne was born. Apparently, her father doted on her."

"Goodness. How did you find all that out?"

"From old newspapers. Captain Cogdill and one of her brothers visited Suzanne in early 1859. His ship docked in Wilmington for repairs. It was quite an event. Balls and parties honored them—from Beaufort to Savannah. They stayed three months. Their ship suffered major damage in a storm and needed a complete overhaul."

"This project has certainly captured your interest, Mother. Don't you become discouraged when the trail grows cold?"

In spite of herself, Connie admired her mother. She had friends whose parents wiled away their days in nursing homes, waiting for the next meal or Bingo game. Hers had spent the morning researching old records and being shot at.

"Heavens no, dear. That's what keeps it exciting. You just dig a little deeper. I've been thinking, though. If I run out of leads, your father and I may travel to England in July. Perhaps if we visited Dover—where Suzanne grew up and returned after the Civil War—I might learn more. But I couldn't help with your party on Turtle Nest. Could you spare me?"

Yes! thought Connie. But she was genuinely excited for her parents. "That's a wonderful idea, Mother. You and Dad have always talked about going to Europe. Go now while you have your health. And I still have my sanity." She muttered the last under her breath.

"We'll see. By the way. Have you considered dating Robin Benson?"

"What?" Connie dropped the coffee cup she held. It shattered on the kitchen floor.

"Come now, Connie. I'm seventy-five years old, but I'm not blind. Robin dotes on you. Every time he's around you he acts like a tongue-tied schoolboy. When we're on our excursions, he talks about you constantly—your accomplishments, your bright mind, the skillful way you handled Pauline DuVall. I told him every detail of your childhood, including the time you ran down Main Street in my underwear."

"Mother, you didn't!"

"He laughed hardest at that. Consider it, Connie. Growing old is no fun. Growing old alone would be terrifying."

"What do you know about growing old?" Connie tried to alter the focus of conversation. "Let me tell...."

"Don't change the subject," her mother chided. "Besides, I believe I've noticed a spark of interest on your part."

"For Heaven's sakes." Another of Robin's expressions slipped into her dialogue. "He's younger than I am."

"He's forty-six. I asked him today. That's only three years difference—inconsequential."

"Approach Joe slowly," Robin told Helen the next afternoon. "Talk about the camellias, admire his gardenias, ask his advice on pruning your azaleas. I've told him why you're coming. But if you jump in and start asking questions about Nettie Mae, he'll clam up. He'll mention his great-grandmother when he's ready. The whole family protects the old woman. They don't want people exploiting or making fun of her."

"That'll be easy, Robin. I love the garden. I understand St. Bettina's also boasts quite a bird population."

"That's another of Joe's loves. He's put feeders and birdbaths throughout the gardens. He'll talk for hours on that one subject."

Robin introduced Helen to a handsome young black man. Joe Johnston held a biology degree from East Carolina University in Greenville, North Carolina. He could have attended medical school or worked for several large pharmaceutical companies. Instead he returned to Southport as a teacher at the local high school. "Students need good science teachers," Joe once told Robin. "Often the biology teacher would rather coach football. But where will we get our doctors, our environmentalists, our researchers if young people shun the sciences?" This necessitated the second job at St. Bettina's. A schoolteacher's salary would not feed Joe, his wife, and their small children. For his part, Robin was glad. Joe had transformed the gardens into a showplace.

At first, Robin trailed behind Helen and Joe as they walked the grounds admiring blooms and worrying over fledgling shoots. He soon realized he was in the way and excused himself for work in his office. Occasionally, he looked out and saw they had progressed only a few feet from where they had been standing a half-hour before. He quit checking.

At five o'clock, Helen entered his office and propped her feet on a small footstool. "I'm bushed. But what a fascinating afternoon. The man could be a college professor instead of a high school biology teacher. I've never met anyone who knew more about the flora and fauna of eastern North Carolina."

"Did you talk about Nettie Mae?"

"Yes. He finally mentioned her about five minutes ago. He's taking me down there next Thursday afternoon. Just me. You and Connie can't go."

"Helen. I can't agree to that. It could be dangerous. And Connie would never allow it."

"Pooh. Connie needs to remember who changed her diapers. I am going—and alone. Now I must go home. We're going to Calabash for seafood tonight." Helen rose, kissed Robin on the cheek, and left.

The following Thursday, Joe collected Helen and headed to Nettie Mae's. Robin and Connie waited in her cottage. Robin stopped his pacing and regarded Connie. "Don't worry. Joe will take care of your mother. I would never let her go if I thought otherwise." Nevertheless, they jumped at every sound and made nervous small talk until they heard Joe's car.

"Good-bye, Joe. Thanks for a lovely afternoon." Helen waved to her new friend as if they were returning from getting ice cream, rather than a visit to a voodoo queen. She ran up the steps like a girl of eighteen.

"Well?" Robin spoke to her with the voice of a father grilling a daughter after her first date.

"Well, what? Let me catch my breath and I'll fill you in."

Connie brought her mother iced tea on the deck. "I'm afraid there's not much to tell. Joe is a fascinating person, so knowledgeable. He calls Nettie Mae 'G.G.', for 'great-grandmother.'

"G.G. was cordial, but not overly friendly. Joe acted as sort of an interpreter. Nettie Mae speaks the old tongue—almost Gullah speech. I understood little of what she said."

"Did Nettie Mae know about undetectable potions for poisoning people? Had she heard of such a thing being used on a wealthy slave owner?" Robin's curiosity ran rampant. Connie's, too, piqued in anticipation.

"There are indeed such brews," said Helen. "Another possibility is a mixture that induces heart attack. Precipitated by this concoction, death appears natural. Nettie Mae said she'd heard stories of the old slaves poisoning each other—a jealous lover or mad husband—but never of a white person using it. Her great-aunt was the famous voodoo queen Alethia, who reigned at the height of her power when John Marshburn was alive. Alethia taught Nettie Mae all she knows. And she asked about you, Connie."

"Me? How strange. How would she know me?"

"I don't know. But she asked about my daughter—and the color of your hair."

"Spooky." Connie changed the subject. "Where do you go from here?"

"Nowhere, I'm afraid. I've reached the end of my research." Helen sighed, then brightened. "But I talked to your father last night. We're leaving for England on Friday. I'll continue the trail over there."

Hallelujah, thought Connie. But she said, "Isn't that rather sudden?"

"My dear, at our age, sudden is the stuff of heart attacks and strokes. Now is all we have. Make hay while the sun shines and all that!"

Chapter 8

Surprises

Robin surprised Connie by calling the next week, inviting her to the Hungry Pelican—her favorite restaurant. His tone was brusque, businesslike. "I'd like to review my speech for the Turtle Nest party with you," he offered as reason for the invitation.

Socializing with the priest held little appeal. She still wanted distance from any aspect of religion. Her mother's hints, coupled with her own questions, stifled any rational judgment of her relationship with Robin. But she thought of no convenient excuse, so accepted. Besides, she'd felt so blue lately. Maybe she should go out.

He arrived promptly at seven o'clock. When Connie greeted the priest, she found the same shy, ill-at-ease klutz she'd encountered at their first meeting. He stood at her door, red-faced and embarrassed, staring at his feet. *Oh dear,* she thought. *This may be a long evening.*

Robin was dressed casually for dinner. Connie supposed priests had little choice in wardrobe, their clerical collars bolted around their neck upon graduation from seminary. Beneath his collar he wore a black short-sleeved shirt and khaki trousers—his lean, muscular body barely concealed under the modest clothes. *Not bad,* the sensual part of her being judged before the prim, proper self regained control. Robin was an athlete as well as a priest. She often passed him as he jogged the streets of Southport. And she knew he starred on the church baseball team.

Connie had given little thought to her outfit. In the past, she shopped for clothes and took great pains with her wardrobe. Lately, she didn't care—another example of the listlessness that pervaded every aspect of her life. Tonight she chose the first clean garment she found in her closet—a black, A-lined mini-dress embroidered with large coral flowers. The dark background set off her tan while the dress accentuated her figure. "You look lovely," Robin mumbled, helping her into his car. The tension never left his voice, but the shyness somehow endeared him.

"I recommend Andy's Stuffed Clams," Robin said as he seated her. "I ate here last week and they were delicious." They sat alone in the restaurant, their table overlooking the pier and ocean beneath. A full moon shone yellow on the breaking waves. Connie pondered the incongruity of conducting a business meeting in such a romantic setting.

His recommendation of the clams proved a mouth-watering choice. Served in their own shells, they were moist and sweet. "I'm almost a vegetarian," she told him. "But I could never give up seafood."

They discussed his upcoming talk. Robin mapped out his speech for Connie. She added a few ideas—points to entice the legislators for support of the restoration project and the entire region, including Turtle Nest. But Robin was a gifted speaker. He needed little help.

Robin remained nervous and preoccupied throughout the meal. Something troubled the priest—something unrelated to his upcoming speech. Connie caught him staring at her if she glanced away—the open hunger on his face quickly masked when she looked back. *What is going on with this man? I can't remember a meal when my dinner partner seemed so preoccupied.*

After discussing his speech and progress on the church restoration, Connie amused Robin with her parent's latest exploits. "They left for England last Friday. Dad was beside himself. Mother packed eleven suitcases and they're only staying two weeks—not two months!"

Her depression lifted as they talked. In spite of his nervousness, Robin charmed her with amusing stories from his years in seminary. His presence was calming, yet the erotic sensations she'd felt earlier continued to tease.

The moon that poured forth light at the beginning of their meal now huddled—subdued and sedate—in a remote corner of the sky. The waiter lingered each time he came to their table, staring at them as if to convey a pointed message. The restaurant was closing. They left, feeling like children who stayed too late at the party.

On her doorstep, Robin gave no indication of saying goodnight, but held the door open and followed her in. For lack of an alternative, she suggested they watch the waning moon over her deck.

Connie poured them each a glass of white wine and settled back as the last of the moonbeams shone across the marsh. "Even though tomorrow is Saturday, I've got a busy day," she prompted. "I can't sit here too long."

Robin chose a chair nearby, accidentally brushing her arm as he passed. He jumped at the contact. Connie, too, flinched with sensation. The hard muscle of his calf brought to mind the rest of his body—strong, fit, primed for pleasure. They sat in silence, each acutely aware of the other's presence.

Staring at his large hands, he struggled with a thought, then spoke. "I'm sorry. I'm being a bit of a clod. You must wonder what's going on. Obviously, I have my speech well planned. That was a thin excuse for going out this evening."

"I had wondered," murmured Connie.

"The truth is, well ..." Even in the shadowy half-light, Connie saw him blush. "I'm a man who preaches to his congregation every Sunday. I counsel people on living their lives. Yet I'm making an awful mess of this."

"Spit it out, Robin. I find that's best. We'll sort it through when you're finished."

"I ... well ... I was wondering if you would consider seeing me on a ... a social basis."

"A social basis?" His formality confused her.

"Well, ah, yes. You know. Go out—date."

"Oh." Tongue-tied, Connie stammered in confusion. *Now what? Robin attracted her, but dating ...?* And except for her mother's hints, she knew nothing of Robin's feelings.

"I know I'm not as rich or handsome or exciting as some of the men you meet. But we seem to enjoy each other's company. I find you a very attractive woman. And your mother encouraged me and gave me hope." Once Robin opened the floodgates, words gushed forth like water over a giant dam.

"Oh." Connie repeated. They sat in silence watching a great night bird fly low over the marsh, then disappear. The evening air caressed their bodies like a soft blanket—thrown wide to trap them in this moment in time.

What could it hurt? She admitted to herself that she enjoyed Robin's company. Tonight she felt relaxed and if not happy, at least less blue. For weeks the question of her true feelings for him had rattled around in her brain. Maybe she wouldn't know the answer until she asked the question. Wasn't there a song to that effect?

Robin finally broke the silence. Rising, he said, "I'm sorry if I offended you." Her silence had spoken volumes.

She reached out her hand and stopped him. "No. I'm the one who should apologize. Sitting here like a bashful preteen. You took me by surprise, that's all. The truth is, I don't know how I feel. I admit I'm attracted to you. Beyond that, I don't know. But if you're interested in exploring a relationship on that basis, then so am I.

"I don't do that much dating. Usually, I scare men off. I think they're afraid of a woman who owns her own business. Would that be a problem for you—to date a woman who's independent? I warn you. I do things my own way. I can be aggressive and hard-nosed, and I don't usually ask for another opinion. Could you deal with that? I'm too set in my ways to change."

Robin jumped up and gave her a robust handshake. *How strange,* she thought. *Especially after someone agreed to date you.*

"Oh Connie. That would be wonderful. What more could I ask? And yes, I most definitely can accept your independence. That's one reason I'm attracted to you. I'm tired of women who can't think for themselves."

He left soon after, sauntering down the walk like a twelve year old who'd gotten his first kiss. At the end of the sidewalk, he actually leaped over her gate.

"Thanks, Mom," whispered Connie, not knowing whether or not she meant it.

They began dating casually—usually on weekends. In Southport the single theater showed out-of-date movies. Last week they had driven to Wilmington to see the latest *Star Wars* film. As often as not, their date consisted of a trip to the local hardware store seeking some supply for a repair job at Connie's house. Then Robin returned and fixed the errant board or pipe.

Once Robin laughed and told her, "The ladies at St. Bettina's are in a quandary. They don't know if we're serious or not. One asked that question point blank after church last Sunday, but I brushed her off."

Connie didn't know either. But she liked the situation. Robin was easy to be with—interesting, but silent if the occasion warranted. Unlike other suitors, he felt no need to impress with his knowledge or business acumen.

She found she missed him when they were separated—saving tidbits of her day to share with him. This need for companionship was new to her. She'd always been content by herself, feeling superior to women who clung to a man.

Their date tonight, if it could be called a date, took place on Connie's deck. They shared a bottle of chardonnay and watched dusk settle over the marsh.

Tonight a new moon, a tiny silver slice, hung over them. They leaned against the rail and counted sand crabs hurrying to their holes.

"What do you hear from your mother, Connie? Has she solved the mystery of Suzanne Marshburn?"

"Oh, Robin. You won't believe it." Connie groaned. "I got a letter from her yesterday. She found Suzanne's home in Dover. The Duchess of Leicester owns it. She lives there alone, except for her servants.

"Everyone told Mother the duchess was a recluse and she'd never meet her. But Mom marched up to the old home and rang the doorbell." Connie quoted her mother's letter. "'She grows beautiful roses in her courtyard. I thought I'd just go up and compliment her.'"

"Has the duchess shed any light on the mystery?"

"Not yet. But she invited Mother to high tea next week. Mother will broach the subject then."

"Your mother is an amazing woman, Connie. She takes after her daughter." Robin rested one arm across her shoulders. Now he turned to her, cupping her face in his hands.

He had kissed her before—gentle Sunday school pecks. This time a new look illuminated his face. A hunger. He gathered her in his arms and kissed her deeply. His tongue explored the secret places of her mouth. Tentatively, she returned the favor. A tingle at the base of her spine spread downward through more remote regions of her body. The Unseen that often intruded on her intimate moments hovered in the background. Connie wanted to keep it there.

"Whoa," she gasped, pulling away from him and resting her head on his chest. "I didn't know clergy kissed like that."

"I'm a priest, not a monk," murmured Robin. They stayed like this for some moments, Robin stroking her cheek and Connie resting in the arms of this good man.

Again she thought how comfortable, how light-hearted she felt with him. But was that enough? Tonight proved there might be more than she'd imagined—a passion that met his and fulfilled itself in wild abandon.

"Connie," Robin broke into her thoughts. "Thank you for these last few weeks. I've had more fun, felt more joy, than I've known in a long time."

In response, Connie stretched her arms around his waist and held him. Soon he kissed her lightly and left.

CHAPTER 9

▼

OLD BONES

Friday morning found Robin working frantically in the church office. He'd procrastinated on his sermon all week. Now he must sit down and write. Sunday was only two days away. He hated forcing the words. Better to let the Spirit flow through you and onto the paper. But he knew that was the exception, rather than the norm. God probably wanted him to sweat for his bread like everyone else.

"Father Robin, Father Robin! Come quickly!" Robin looked up and saw Joe Johnston banging on the screen door. Robin leaped from his desk and threw the door open. Steadying Joe by the arm, he helped him into the room.

"What is it Joe? Are you hurt? I told you not to cut those limbs until—"

"No. Oh, no. I'm not hurt." Joe eased into a chair and gasped for breath. Though young, Joe had run from the gardens to the church office.

"Rest here, Joe. Let me get you some water." When Robin returned he rested a hand on Joe's heaving shoulder and gave him the glass.

The gardener gulped the water, gagging on the last swallow. He trembled with excitement, choking as he tried to form words.

Robin clasped the sweat-soaked shoulder. "Take your time. Tell me when you're able."

After several attempts, Joe gasped. "I-I found graves. Unmarked graves. At the far end of the church property. You remember I told you I was moving that white camellia this morning? I started digging. About an hour ago. I needed a big hole because it's a huge old bush. But I didn't get far before I started uncovering bones. At first I thought I'd discovered a dog's stockpile. But I kept finding more. Then I realized they were human bones. That's when I quit digging and came for you."

"You're mistaken, Joe. There are no gravestones in that part of the churchyard. Old church maps show no graves there. It's been abandoned for years. That's why we're moving the camellia. With the restoration of St. Bettina's we should reclaim the area."

"I know. They're human remains, though. I'm sure of what I saw. Anyone who's seen a skeleton on Halloween could identify those bones."

Robin shook his head in disbelief. He'd walked those grounds thousands of times. He'd know if unidentified graves were on the property.

Joe paused before adding, "There's one more thing."

"What's that?" Robin asked.

Joe shook his head sadly. "Some of the skeletons wear leg irons. Fetters—engraved with a sheaf of rice. The initials "JAM" are stamped beneath."

At Joe's suggestion, Robin contacted Dr. John Beard of East Carolina University. Dr. Beard taught archeology and was an expert in forensics. He had been Joe's professor when Joe was a student at East Carolina. Robin also notified town authorities and asked that the area be secured.

"Stopping the digging is wise, Father Benson," Dr. Beard said over the telephone. "This indicates an important archeological find—for St. Bettina's and all of eastern North Carolina. In addition to the human remains, we may find artifacts. Toys, buttons, eating utensils, and pottery often lodge in old graves. I'll come to Southport tomorrow. In the meantime, see what you can learn about those leg irons marked with the rice sheaf and initials."

Instead of finishing his sermon, Robin spent the afternoon in the public library researching old marks and brands. *Oh well,* he rationalized, *maybe I can find a sermon in this.*

His search floundered until four o'clock when Hattie O'Brien entered the library. A spinster and the local, self-appointed expert on Civil War history, Hattie spent her days studying the era and holding office in the United Daughters of the Confederacy. She talked of little else.

"Father Benson. I must tell you what my precious niece Elizabeth said the other day. You know she's just nine years old and already belongs to the Junior Daughters of the Confederacy. Anyway, she came home from last Thursday's meeting furious with me. 'Aunt Hattie,' she fussed, putting her hands on her hips and stomping her foot, 'You never told me we lost the war!'"

"To hear you talk, Miss Hattie, we didn't." Robin genuinely admired the old lady, appreciating her strong spirit and sharp mind. It occurred to him she might know something about the leg irons.

"Oh dear me, yes, Father Robin," she declared when Robin showed her a sketch of the rice sheaf and initials. "That brand was prominent in this area in 1850. The rice sheaf symbolized the rice plantation, Marshlands, located a few miles upriver. And the initials belonged to its owner, John Ames Marshburn.

"His wife, Suzanne, was quite a beauty, you know. And a dear friend of Rose O'Neal Greenhow, the Confederate spy. We named our local chapter of the United Daughters of the Confederacy for Mrs. Greenhow, The Rose O'Neal Greenhow Chapter. Such a brave woman, so dedicated. You know she died right here off the coast of Southport. Drowned, trying to...."

Robin loved Hattie, but knew better than to let her ramble on about the Confederacy or her local chapter of the UDC. Apologizing with the excuse that his sermon needed attention, he hurriedly left the library.

The next morning, Robin eagerly waited for Dr. Beard at the church cemetery. When the professor arrived and jumped from his Jeep, Robin encountered a man much younger than he'd expected. The trim black beard outlined the face of a man barely thirty.

"Welcome, Professor Beard. Since you were Joe's professor, I expected a much older man. Someone needing help to the gravesites."

Dr. Beard laughed. His bright blue eyes shone with intelligence and friendship. Robin liked him at once. "I'm an assistant professor, actually. But thanks for the compliment. Please call me John. Joe and I are the same age. He got a late start and I went from college straight through graduate school. Where is Joe, anyway?"

"He's at the gravesite. Doing some gardening so he can spend time with us. I'll take you there."

Robin escorted John Beard down the old brick walk, then across the mossy church yard. Their feet squished on fallen pine needles as they climbed a small knoll to the secluded gravesite.

Joe was till struggling with the out-of-place camellia. Pleasure flooded his face when he rested on his spade and saw his former professor. He greeted Dr. Beard with a bear hug. Robin stood aside and compared the two men—both quiet and reserved, but fiercely interested in their scientific pursuits. He let them catch up on personal news before intruding.

After several minutes, Robin grasped the professor's arm and escorted him to a grave. Outlining a perimeter with a sweep of his hand, he began his explanation. "These are the gravesites, John. Actually it's more like a mass grave. It's a real puzzle why so many people are buried together. But we solved the mystery of the leg irons."

Robin detailed the information he'd learned from Harriet O'Brien—that the leg irons belonged to plantation owner John Ames Marshburn.

The professor examined the bones. "Of course we will do a thorough excavation. As I told you, this is an important archeological find. From what you've said, these bones date from at least 130 years ago. I'll bring students down on Monday and we'll begin right away.

"Look at the lesions on this leg. That's muscle torn from bone—caused by strain and overwork. These circular fractures at the base of this skull? The result of heavy loads carried on shoulders or head. In this case it looks like that's what caused death. See the spine pushed into the cranial cavity? Someone drove these slaves unmercifully. Even the children worked to the edge of human capacity—and they were malnourished. There's a trove of information in these bones, none of it pretty."

Robin picked up the thin forearm of a child, holding it in his palm with the same reverence he bestowed on the communion cup. Tears filled his eyes. "We know John Marshburn whipped his slaves. That's how he died. But this speaks of continual ill treatment."

Dr. Beard wrapped the exposed bones in cloth, laid them gently in the grave, and then smoothed dirt over the mound. "As I said, we'll begin our investigation on Monday."

"Should we halt our restoration project until you finish?"

"Oh no. We'll excavate for quite a while. Maybe a year, off and on. This spot is secluded enough for us to stay out of your way—and you out of ours. Plus we must notify the authorities in Raleigh. They will probably check on us periodically. There's one more thing, though."

"What's that?"

"There may be media coverage. Discoveries of this kind make sensational news. And it could get ugly, since it involves the mistreatment of human beings. Are you prepared for that?"

"I think we can handle it, maybe even turn it into good, as a lesson on the immorality of enslaving others and as advertisement for our restoration project."

But Robin was astounded by the sudden and vehement reaction to the discovery. By Sunday, everyone in Southport knew about the graves. The pews at St. Bettina's filled for the first time since Easter. Robin chided himself for not polishing his sermon. After the service and for the rest of the afternoon, a steady stream of gawkers trickled through the churchyard.

As they patrolled the perimeter of the gravesites, Sheriff Nat McLeod and his deputy had become instant experts. "Stay back ladies and gentlemen, you're looking at an important historical find. Now what really happened here was that...."

On Monday a reporter from the Southport paper greeted Dr. Beard and his students on their arrival at the archeological site. The next day, hungry reporters and television crews from Wilmington descended on the scene. By Wednesday, media from Raleigh, Charlotte, even Asheville came. The restaurants and motels rejoiced.

Joe Johnston grumbled. "Those fools scare the birds and tramp all over the garden, Robin. You know that ancient magnolia by the fence?"

"The one that's almost as old as the church?"

"That's the one. This morning I found a photographer hanging from a branch, shooting aerial photos of the grave. When I insisted he get down, he cursed."

"Patience, Joe. This too shall pass."

But Robin's assurances proved false. Instead of lessening, excitement over the burial grounds grew. After the media carried the news throughout the Southeast, visitors came from as far away as Tennessee, Kentucky, even Texas. African-Americans seeking roots, college students looking for a thrill, Mom and Pop in the RV, all descended on the tiny churchyard.

The only bright spot occurred when Robin was able to ease Joe's continued grumbling about the visitors. "Build a collection box, Joe. Make yourself a little sign saying 'Donations for the Upkeep of the Graves' or 'Help Feed the Birds.' Put your box where visitors can't miss it."

Joe constructed his box in the shape of a bluebird house and positioned it at the entrance to the gravesite. The results thrilled him. "I collected twenty-five dollars today, Robin. Now I can buy the fertilizer I need. How'd you think up such a great idea?"

"In seminary. Fundraising 101. The chapter titled 'Collecting Money When Your Parishioners Least Expect It.'"

As Robin left his office, he congratulated himself on solving Joe's problem. Turning the key in the lock, he mumbled to the church door, "I handled that pretty well, if I say so myself."

Later, Robin remembered the adage "Pride goeth before a fall." Lost in self-congratulation, he failed to see the wires and equipment scattered across the church steps or the television crew waiting for his appearance.

Bombarded by the bright lights of a monstrous, three-eyed camera, Robin swayed in confusion. Without prelude, the sandpaper-rough voice of a reporter assaulted him.

"Father Benson. Good morning. I'm Jack Tully, WXXT News, Raleigh. Is it true work on the restoration of St. Bettina's continues, in spite of the discovery of the slave burial grounds?" Tully thrust his microphone in Robin's face.

The light from the camera blinded Robin. His assailant's face swam in the brightness. Disoriented and confused, he groped for an answer.

"Well, ah, yes. It's true. Delaying our project serves no purpose. Dr. James Beard from East Carolina University is excavating the graves. He assured me that work on both sites, the church and the grave, could proceed simultaneously."

Tully persisted but his face remained hidden, giving Robin the impression of talking to a non-person. "And isn't it also true that Dr. Beard identified the bones as those of slaves belonging to John Ames Marshburn from his plantation Marshlands? And that the remains show definite signs of abuse and mistreatment?"

Robin tensed. The direction of this conversation alarmed him. "Well, ah, yes," he mumbled.

"There you have it folks. It's just as Senator Clarence Roberts, retired United States senator, revealed to us. The restoration committee, headed by Miss Connie Edmonds of Edmonds Land Development Company, is not concerned about the discovery of the burial plot. Soon giant bulldozers, trucks, and excavation equipment will trundle over these grounds, destroying valuable evidence. It will be a disservice to the African-American descendants of these slaves. It may even be a crime. Perhaps Miss Edmonds doesn't want the extent of the abuse known. Or perhaps, and this is really sinister, her company might lose money in fees and kickbacks if restoration work slows."

"Just a minute, Tully." Robin interjected. "I made the decision to continue work. Ms. Edmonds had nothing—"

Jack Tully was as adept at ignoring Robin as he had been in accosting him. The reporter turned his back and positioned the bulky camera between himself and Robin. A new subject garnered his attention. "Ladies and gentlemen. What an honor. I see Senator Roberts arriving now. The senator is eighty-five years old but feels so strongly about this desecration that he made the arduous trip from Greensboro. With him is William Avery, prominent leader in the North Carolina Civil Rights movement."

The old senator tottered up the brick walk toward the church, supported by his chauffeur and a handsome black man. William Avery, Robin supposed.

The appearance of the senator shocked him. As a priest, Robin recognized impending death. He knew Roberts was in his eighties. But Connie described him as robust and spry. The skeleton inching up the path would live, at best, a few more months.

When Roberts spoke, however, his voice radiated the fire that, for many years, intimidated opponents in the United States Senate. "Jack, you must stop this sacrilege. Thank goodness you brought a camera crew to Southport so America can see what's happening. I've known Connie Edmonds for years. This is her handiwork—total disrespect for the rights and feelings of others. Anxious to make money, whatever it takes."

Robin couldn't believe what he heard. Jack Tully and his entourage were taking a small bit of truth and completely distorting it. Angrily, he tried to elbow through the barricade of camera, cameraman, and newscaster. Ignoring him, the television crew circumvented his moves. Clarence Roberts continued his barrage in his raspy smoke-damaged voice.

Furious at being ignored, Robin grabbed Jack Tully's shoulder and swung the newscaster around. "Damn it, Tully. Quit broadcasting lies. Let me tell our side of the story." Tully fell against him in an exaggerated stumble. The television camera recorded it all.

"Well, ladies and gentlemen, what have we here? Connie Edmonds' lackey, a priest who curses and attacks the media for telling the truth." Tully rubbed his shoulder for emphasis.

If Tully had bothered to look closely, he would have seen the blue in the priest's eyes change to a cold, steely gray. Balling his fist, Robin swung at the reporter.

At the last moment, William Avery's strong arm blocked Robin's. Twisting the arm behind Robin's back, Avery shoved him from the group and closed the circle.

Avery turned and faced the camera. "Another example, ladies and gentlemen, of a white person using force to quell our story. My fellow African-Americans, speak out! Let your cry be heard! Protest the destruction of your ancestors' gravesite!"

Robin heard no more. Shaken and blinded with anger, he did not protest as one of the camera crew grabbed him and propelled him down the walk toward his car.

Later that evening, Connie and Robin sat on the floor before her television, watching the interview on the eleven o'clock news. "What a fool I made of myself," Robin stormed. "Why didn't I leave and go for help? I look like a complete idiot—standing there cursing and swinging at that lowlife Tully. I'll hear from the bishop on this one."

"Oh, Robin. Don't be so hard on yourself. Anyone would have reacted the way you did."

"Yes, but I'm not anyone. I'm a priest. Priests control their tempers, and their language."

Robin spoke his next words to the floor. He'd never made this confession to anyone except his bishop. But Connie was fast becoming more than just anyone to him.

"Connie," he began. "You must know this about me. I have a terrible temper. I struggle with it daily. Burly Peters and I have discussed this at length. Until I can control my temper, I'm limited in my ability as a priest.

"Most of the time, I come across as shy and unsure of myself. That's true. I am. But often I'm ill at ease because I'm wrestling with emotions I can't tame. That's what happened today. And Tully has just broadcast that to the whole world."

Preoccupied with the unfairness of the situation, Connie missed the depth of Robin's confession. Her attention centered on the false accusations. "It's so unfair, implying that we're desecrating the graves. We're conducting a thorough investigation of the burial plot and honoring the site with a permanent marker. And the insinuation that I'm profiting from this. My company doesn't even do this kind of work. It's another example of Clarence Roberts harassing me and my business."

As an afterthought she added, "You're right. Roberts looks terrible."

Robin abandoned his own problems to deal with the present. "I've telephoned WXXT and complained. I told them the decision to continue work on the project was Dr. Beard's and mine. Neither you, nor anyone else on the board, had input. They've promised me equal time on tomorrow's news. But I'm afraid the damage is done. By tomorrow morning, my ill-aimed swing and Clarence Roberts' face will coat the front page of every newspaper in the Southeast."

"Ugh," Connie grimaced. "What a thing to wake up to."

Robin slipped his arm around Connie's shoulders and kissed away the grimace. "Let's don't talk about Clarence Roberts, lost tempers, dead slaves, or anything unpleasant tonight. This time is just for us." He continued until his kisses changed from friendly teases to deep longings. His arms encircled her and began to caress her breasts, her back, her thighs.

Connie returned the caresses and sensed herself losing touch with reality. Slowly she slipped into the tide of his passion, carried by her own strong feelings. She floated down some warm, dark corridor. Her desire for him rose gradually until it controlled her entire body.

Suddenly, from the depths of Hell, the demon-figure appeared in Connie's corridor. Black shrouds twisted around a gnarled, deformed body. Around its flaccid neck the chain of bright, copper coins jangled with the incessant ringing of an out-of-tune alarm clock.

"Ha! Bitch! What do you think you're doing?" the grotesque face shrieked—pointing, gesturing, laughing a hideous laugh. "What makes you think a man could love you," the shade screamed, its strident cry clashing in discord with the clanging necklace. "You're not worthy of love, you slut. You're trash, you hear me? No good, worthless trash!"

Connie lost any desire for love. Trembling, she broke the embrace, stood, and stumbled to a chair.

"What's wrong, Connie? Don't you love me?" Totally perplexed, Robin moved beside her.

"Oh I do, Robin. I do." Caught off-guard, Connie acknowledged aloud what she'd hidden from herself, the shock of the demon triggering the confession that she loved the priest.

"It's just ... well ... it's hard to explain."

"Please try. Why do you shy away from making love?"

"Oh, Robin. You'll think I'm crazy. But I'm haunted. Haunted by this demon that appears whenever I get close to a man. I think the demon is a woman. Or was a woman, that is, returned from the dead. She's so ugly, all black and misshapen. And she laughs at me. Always she points and mocks and ridicules me. I'm terrified, Robin. Where does she come from?"

Robin thought long about the situation. Finally he answered. "I don't have an answer, Connie. In my business, I counsel people on a variety of subjects. But I've learned from experience that when something scary appears, like what you saw, it's usually your unconscious sending you a message. Sometimes our subconscious mind helps us by scaring us."

"Well that makes no sense."

"No. I know it doesn't. But we understand little about how the mind operates. I do know that your psyche works for good. Maybe it grabs your attention by scaring you."

"It did that—scared me, I mean."

"Let me help you, Connie. Lord knows, it's my profession. Spend the next few days thinking about it. You say it comes when you make love. Why should that scare you? Have you ever been hurt? Abused? Do you feel some tremendous guilt?"

They talked a while longer. Connie served Dilcey's delicious lemon pound cake and coffee. Robin left soon afterward.

"Goodnight, Connie," he whispered, brushing her cheek with his fingers. "Try to rest."

Connie forced a sad smile. "I wish it were that easy." As she closed the door, she felt the gloom of depression settle over her and seep into her soul.

Chapter 10

▼

Steeples and Spires

Lucy ate dinner with Connie again before the monthly meeting of the St. Bettina's board. Tonight they sat at Connie's kitchen table sharing a pepperoni pizza.

"M-m-m, pizza, my favorite food." Lucy talked as she licked gooey cheese from her fingers, twirling it between her thumb and forefinger like a child. "By the way, Charlie and I received our invitation to your party on Turtle Nest. We're thrilled you included friends as well as politicians. How can we help?"

"It's all planned. Janie Kilpatrick did a great job. But once we're on the island you and Charlie can talk up the place, circulate among the legislators and their wives. Be my eyes and ears as to their reaction, see who needs extra persuasion, that sort of thing. The party wouldn't be taking place if it weren't for you." Although still not as enthusiastic as her co-workers, Connie realized that hosting the party was a wise business decision.

"But you and your staff did the work. It'll be easy to praise the island and your development ideas, Connie. Your brochure was beautiful. I love the artist's drawing of the little church with the enormous window overlooking the marsh. It combines the natural with the man-made, enhancing the spirit of worship. Charlie and I may build at Turtle Nest, rather than Morehead."

"My able salespeople will help you," laughed Connie.

"I also liked your itinerary for the day. Having Robin speak was a brainstorm. And we'll enjoy hearing Bill Pace talk about turtle conservation. He's an eloquent man. You know I serve on the board for NCUTE—North Carolina United Turtle Enthusiasts."

"How many boards are you on?" teased Connie. Glancing at her watch, she jumped up and began stuffing leftover pizza into her refrigerator—to Lucy's disappointment.

"We should leave, Luce. I don't want to be late. We're making several major decisions tonight. The most important concerns the church steeple."

"The steeple? Why is that a problem? St. Bettina's' steeple is one of its most beautiful features. It's so tall you can see it from the harbor." As she spoke, Lucy took out her compact, checking her mouth for stray pizza sauce.

"Robin found one architect who suggested removing the spire and capping it about five feet above the roof line with a smaller steeple and cross. That would shorten the tower and do away with the bell, but save $8000. The old steeple is in terrible condition. Essentially, it requires rebuilding."

"Well, I know how I'm voting. Without the original bell tower, St. Bettina's wouldn't be the same." Lucy dropped her compact in her purse and stood up. "Let's go. I don't want to miss this vote."

When Connie and Lucy arrived at the church, they found that the only board member not present was Joshua Dunn, who had sent word that business pressures detained him. Connie called the meeting to order, noticing that Pauline DuVall was fidgeting in her chair. As soon as the minutes were read and the floor opened for business, Pauline's hand was in the air, waving back and forth.

"Madame Chairman," Pauline said when she was recognized, "I don't know if this is old business or new business, but it's something that must be dealt with immediately. I'm talking about the disgraceful publicity we've received since the graves were found on the church property. And the accusations. Our chairwoman may be profiting from all of this. She should resign immediately. She's lining her pockets at the expense of—"

"Just a minute, Mrs. DuVall." Bishop Peters rose to speak, keeping one hand on a furious Robin. "As bishop of this diocese, it's my responsibility to address this sort of situation. Believe me, I already have. I've done a thorough investigation and can tell you that Miss Edmonds, as well as Father Benson, have done nothing wrong. If anything, they have both gone out of their way to respect the gravesites.

"It's not the jurisdiction of this committee to be involved in this issue. We are about renovation—church renovation. My office and the vestry of St. Bettina's deal with publicity and are handling these accusations. I support Miss Edmonds.

A discovery like the one made at St. Bettina's will naturally attract media attention. But that is not our agenda for tonight."

"But—" Pauline began.

"The issue is closed, Mrs. DuVall. We will discuss it no further." Bishop Peters leveled his "fire and brimstone" stare on Pauline. Even she did not dare to continue arguing.

Connie thanked the bishop and continued the meeting. She saved the subject of the steeple for the last item on the agenda. Then she asked Robin to speak.

Slowly the priest rose to present the architect's report. The concern he felt was etched in two deep crevices that dragged down the corners of his mouth. "The capped steeple would be less expensive," he acknowledged. "But can we accept that? Some things have no price. I believe our steeple is one of those."

After Robin sat down, Connie called for a vote. Lucy, as secretary, counted the ballots. "We have three yeas and three nays," she announced.

General argument ensued. "We must save money," Bishop Peters said. "We're already over budget. We've got to draw the line somewhere."

"That's right," agreed Pauline. "We can't spend and spend without being accountable to our parishioners. The steeple offers an excellent opportunity to save a great deal of money."

"I'll give up my new vestments," Robin offered. "That'll save a bundle. And I'm sure we can cut corners in other areas if we look hard enough."

Lucy and Connie took Robin's side. Sims DuVall sat quietly in his chair. No one wondered about his vote.

"We're at an impasse," sighed Connie after requesting a second vote. I'll call Joshua Dunn for his vote—his secretary sent an emergency number." She left the room but returned shortly. "No answer. He must be out. Let's take the vote once more."

Again the decision split. Connie fretted about the situation. It was late and they had made no progress. They could postpone the vote for a month, but that would delay work on the renovation. Besides, she acknowledged, Joshua Dunn would choose the smaller steeple. She had noticed that whichever way she voted, Dunn objected, then took the other course. And the DuValls always followed his lead.

Settling the issue tonight, without Dunn's vote, was Connie's preference. She stared pointedly at the DuValls. "We'll recess for ten minutes. During the break, each of you go off by yourself. Look up at the steeple. Search your souls. Decide if the smaller steeple will truly satisfy you. I understand some of you believe saving money is the best course. Bishop Peters, I realize that you must consider what's best for the entire diocese.

"One of us may change his or her mind. Or we may remain at an impasse. If so, we'll wait until next month. That will delay the project, but it may be our only choice. I'll ring this bell in ten minutes. This will be our last vote for the evening, no matter what the outcome."

Connie watched Pauline leave by the side door and motion for her husband. Sims pretended not to see and let himself out the back. *Interesting,* she thought.

Restless and anxious, Connie paced the room. Finally, overwhelmed by her own emotions, she too went outside. The cool wash of the evening welcomed her and began calming her runaway emotions.

Walking around the side of the church, Connie stared at the bell tower. In the moonlight it looked like a ghostly specter, partially hidden by magnolias and Spanish moss. They couldn't lose it. The steeple comprised the essence of St. Bettina's, its beauty, history, and solidarity.

"Oh Lord, please let us keep it." An involuntary prayer left her lips. Connie was shocked. She hadn't prayed in twenty years.

In her adult life, she'd considered religion a crutch for the weak, those who couldn't make it on their own. But she realized Robin and Lucy drew great strength from their faith. And she knew few men as fine as Bishop Peters. Did they know something she didn't?

"Fiddlesticks," she mumbled. "All this thinking gives me a headache." She stomped back to the meeting room and rang the bell. The members returned promptly, except for Sims DuVall. "I don't know where he is," Pauline whined. "I spent the recess searching for him."

They waited five, ten, fifteen minutes. Connie rang the bell twice more. Finally she prepared to adjourn the meeting. "Mr. DuVall seems to have left. We'll postpone the vote until next month."

As she said this, a breathless Sims DuVall hurried into the room. Life filled his face and flowed out to the other board members. His eyes glistened with the joy of a child hiding a secret. He stood taller now than the shell of a man who had slunk off thirty minutes earlier, hiding from an overbearing wife.

"No, wait," Sims begged. "Please stay. Please vote tonight. My apologies for delaying the meeting. I just wanted to be sure, very sure." He glanced furtively at Pauline. "Madame Chairman, could I address the board before we vote?"

"You have the floor, Mr. DuVall. But please be brief. We're already running overtime."

"Thank you, Madame Chairman. Again, my apologies." His formality amused Connie. But then, when had Sims said more than two words to her? And always in Pauline's presence. She realized she knew little about the man.

The wispy, balding hardware salesman stood at his place and spoke. Not looking at the group, he conversed quietly with the aluminum table. As he talked his voice gained strength. He raised his head and looked each committee member in the eye—except for his wife. The gladness infusing Sims' face was infectious. Robin stretched out his legs and unclenched his fists. Lucy smiled encouragement. Pauline, however, was staring at her husband with open mouthed amazement.

"I did what Miss Edmonds asked of us. I wandered off alone and thought about the steeple. There's a hollow tree down in the old Smithville Burial Ground. As a boy, I hid there for privacy and solace. Spooky, yes. But who'll bother you in a cemetery?

"Anyway, I sat there and looked at the steeple as I did many years ago. I remembered how I came here with my boyhood problems. I drew comfort from that spire. It symbolized my connection to God. A lightening rod, if you will. Sometimes I was angry with Him and complained. Other times I'd implore. But His message always flowed through the steeple—one of love, comfort, and peace.

"As an adult, I never thought much about it. But tonight I realized that I still draw strength from the bell tower. You can see it from any point in Southport. If I face a tricky business situation, difficult problem, or am just tired, I unconsciously glance at it and feel uplifted.

"My friends, we cannot destroy the steeple. If it means this much to me, many folks must feel the same way. Not just Episcopalians, but people from all walks of life. I'm sure it inspires tourists passing by on their boats. They see it as a white arrow pointing toward the sky. They hear the melodious tolling of our bell. For some, it may be their only message that God watches over them.

"A church steeple is more than boards, nails, and figures on a balance sheet. It's an edifice, a symbol, reaching to heaven like people shaking their finger at God, or touching His face—then receiving His blessing in return."

By now Sims was perspiring and trembling. He sat down shakily and dropped his head in his hands. But he had given something to the board members. Something related to hope, happiness, and a sense of continuity between past and future.

Connie glanced around the room. Tears filled the eyes of several committee members. When Pauline recovered her voice, she reached over and patted Sims' arm. "Honeypot that was beautiful, just beautiful. You were so ... so eloquent."

"Shall we take our final vote of the evening?" Connie called attention to the question at hand.

Again she, Lucy, and Robin voted for keeping the steeple. Pauline joined her husband in voting "yes." The bishop raised his hands and sighed. "Let's make it unanimous. How can I argue with a speech like that? The man belongs in the pulpit. So it'll mean a few extra bake sales. I'll bring my famous bishop's fruit cake."

"Ugh," moaned Robin. "I can't face the thought of that tonight. Let's go home."

As Connie walked out, she saw Pauline and Sims leaving arm and arm. They giggled like young lovers. "I'll fix your tonic when we get home, Simsy and then …" Shuddering, Connie imagined how the sentence ended.

On Thursday, a surprise visitor appeared at Connie's office. Maggie buzzed, saying a Mrs. Pauline DuVall waited in the reception room. Connie wondered what she wanted. Pauline had never acted friendly toward her. Not since she had learned Connie's family raised pigs. Maybe Sims had changed his mind about the steeple. Maybe Pauline had forced him to.

When Pauline entered, Connie knew that wasn't the case. Pauline lowered her head and inched into the room like a puppy that isn't allowed in the house, but comes in anyway. She eased her great frame onto the edge of a rigidly straight chair and whispered. "I've come to apologize, Miss Edmonds. Apologize, and warn you."

"Surely you'll call me Connie, Pauline."

"All right … Connie." The big woman struggled with her thoughts. Connie still smelled Orange Blossom, but not as overpowering as in the past.

"First, let me apologize for my behavior. I've searched my soul and my dear, sweet Simsy-pooh"—Connie cringed at the endearment—"pointed out a few things. Truth is, I haven't been very nice to you. I've been a snob.

"I think I'm jealous of you. We're about the same age and you're so pretty and self-assured and run your own business and I'm, well …" Pauline gestured toward the body that overflowed her chair.

"But a good man loves me. That's all I need. And I'm doing something about this lard mass I've become. Please forgive me for the way I've treated you."

"There's nothing to forgive, Pauline. Friendliness wasn't my strong suit, either. But let's start over. After all we're restoring a church together."

"Yes we are. And that's why I'm warning you. Joshua Dunn is not your friend, Connie. He's a bitter enemy."

"That's impossible. I hardly know the man."

"True. But you do know Senator Clarence Roberts, don't you?"

Connie groaned. "Unfortunately."

"Dunn is Roberts' lackey, his spy. When Roberts learned you served on the board, he pulled strings to have one of his flunkies appointed too. It was all legitimate. Dunn is a powerful businessman in his own right, but he takes his orders from Roberts.

"I don't know why the senator hates you, Connie. But Dunn's job is to watch you, harass you, and make your life as miserable as possible. Then he reports to Roberts."

"How do you know all this?"

"Dunn enlisted our support early on. At first it sounded like a lark. We didn't know you and he convinced us—me, at least—that you were a cold, calculating, power-hungry ... well, he used the term 'bitch.'

"And," Pauline hung her head. Connie could barely hear her next words. "He promised he'd submit our names as delegates to the next Democratic National Convention. Sims comes from a good family. But we've not important, really. I put on airs pretending otherwise. I thought if we served in the state Democratic party, people would finally look up to us. Please forgive me, Connie."

"I do. Of course I do. But what were you and Sims supposed to do, Pauline?" The extent of Clarence Roberts' influence never ceased to amaze her.

"Spy on you. Block your leadership. Act inattentive at meetings. And always vote with Dunn. He figured if the three of us composed a block, chances were at least one other person would vote with us. He embraced no great vision for the restoration of the church. We were just to find out which way you were leaning and oppose you.

"It would have worked, too, with the steeple, if Dunn had been there. Bishop Peters agreed with us. Joshua didn't know that vote was coming up. None of us did."

"It wasn't a secret. We just reached that point in the restoration and Robin presented the architect's report."

"I know. But if Dunn had voted, the outcome would have been different. An emergency order from Roberts demanded his attention. When Roberts speaks, Dunn jumps. That's why we couldn't reach him by phone.

"I don't know what Roberts wanted of Joshua. It must have been important if it caused him to miss the meeting. Be careful, Connie."

Chapter 11

▼

Breakdown

After Pauline left, Connie found she couldn't concentrate on her work. Pauline's revelations were proof that Roberts enlisted the aid of others for her harm. How often had that happened over the years? She'd never snared a government contract. Now she knew why. The extent of Roberts' influence astounded her.

"Good-bye, Maggie," she mumbled absent-mindedly, gathering her purse and leaving the office.

On the drive home, Connie thought of little except Roberts' persecution. She followed the route to her house by rote. Once inside, she mindlessly began her evening chores. Katie paid her no mind. She was satisfied. She had her supper.

Before leaving for work, Connie had decided on fish for supper. Now she took the flounder from the freezer and turned it in her hands. What should she do with this? Wrapping it in a paper towel, she put it in the microwave, setting the timer for thirty seconds.

Wandering into the bathroom, she stood bewildered in the middle of the floor. Why was she here? She looked around, rearranged a few objects, and then backed from the room. After carefully turning off the lights, she shut the door.

Back in the kitchen, Connie stooped to pet Katie. "Pre-tty, Kit-ty." She caressed the cat in long, slow sweeps. Accustomed to quick pats and fast chatter, Katie looked up quizzically.

The microwave buzzer sounded. Retrieving the fish, Connie stared at it. Now what? The wet, partially thawed mass dripped on the kitchen floor. Wrapping another paper towel around her dinner, she crossed the room to her potted plants. After digging a small trench in the largest, she buried the fish in the dirt.

Connie returned to the bathroom. Why was she back in here? She couldn't remember, so again doused the lights and shut the door.

Standing in the middle of the kitchen floor, Connie studied her fingers. She wore two rings, an antique diamond and an emerald. The diamond flashed in the fluorescent light but the emerald gave off its own inner glow. Slipping them off, she stared at them. Pretty. Shiny. She crossed the room to Katie's litter box. Again she dug a small trench, burying both rings in the gritty compost.

As Connie began her third aimless walk to the bathroom, the doorbell rang. A man's profile silhouetted the windowpane beside her front door. Robin. Why was he here?

She meandered across the room and opened the door. "Come in, Robin. What can I do for you?"

"Don't you remember, Connie? As chairwoman of our board, your signature is required for construction of our new steeple. You said I could bring the papers over tonight."

"Oh, yes. I remember. I think. Come in." As Robin entered, Connie drew an imaginary line on the carpet where she stood. "Don't cross the threshold."

"What? What a strange thing to say. What's the matter with you?" Robin noticed Connie's slurred speech and languid movements.

"Nothing. Nothing at all. Come sit at the kitchen table."

Robin eyed Connie quizzically, then crossed the kitchen and eased into a ladder-back chair at her breakfast table.

"Here. Put your feet under the table. Sit up straight. And rest your hands in your lap."

"Connie. You're acting really weird. Is this some kind of joke?"

"I'm fine, Robin. Sit still. I'll sign the work order. Then let me tell you about my visit from Pauline DuVall."

Connie did seem all right for the rest of the evening. Except for the robot-like speech and sluggish movements, there was no more strange behavior.

Robin left at ten o'clock. As he told Connie goodnight, he put his hands on her shoulders and searched her face. "I know what Pauline said upset you, Connie. The extent of Clarence Roberts' influence staggers the imagination. But he can no longer hurt you through Pauline. She promised that. Go to bed. Stay home from work tomorrow. You need some rest."

"I'm fine, I tell you. Staying home is not possible." Again she drew an imaginary line with her toe. "Don't cross the threshold."

Shaking his head, Robin let himself out as Connie turned and wandered back to the bathroom.

Connie slept little and rose at 5:00 A.M. Remembering Robin's admonition, she scoffed. "If I stayed home every time I missed a night's sleep, I'd never work." Of late, she slept only two or three hours each night.

She arrived at her office well before other staff members. Maggie glanced in at 8:30 to see Connie attacking a stack of papers like an out-of-control fiend. Several contracts needed signing today, bids the company had submitted on three construction projects. All had been accepted. Now Connie studied the paperwork the lawyers had sent.

Maggie left her alone until 11:00. Connie usually broke for tea in midmorning, but today the secretary heard nothing. Curious, she tiptoed to the large office and tapped on the door. Receiving no answer, she pushed the door open, almost knocking her employer to the floor.

"Goodness. I'm sorry—Connie. Gross. What on earth are you doing? You've got dead bugs all over your desk." As a horrified Maggie watched, Connie deposited an insect with the collection already aligned on her desk.

"Just straightening up a bit. The cleaning service does a really lousy job. Here are the contracts, all finished. You can send them back to the lawyers for final approval."

"But Connie, they're all signed in red. I can't mail them like this."

Connie looked at her blankly, then answered mechanically. "They're okay. Send them out."

"But ..." Maggie stood indecisively in the doorway.

"Now go. I'm working." Connie shut the door on her secretary as she bent to retrieve another bug.

Shocked, Maggie stood in front of the closed door. Connie always conducted her affairs in such a predictable, businesslike manner. Sure, the failure of Turtle Nest depressed her. But this behavior bordered on the bizarre.

"What's wrong, Maggie? You look like you've seen a ghost." Tom Crouton approached, carrying a thick file.

"I have. The ghost of Connie. She's lost it, Tom. She's in her office, picking dried insects off the floor. And she signed these legal documents with red ink. Plus she's talking and moving like she's in some sort of trance."

"Oh. She's probably just fooling around. This will bring her to her senses—more information on Clarence Roberts. One of our researchers turned up a juicy little story about Roberts and the wife of a former Speaker of the House."

"Well, good luck. I think she's bonkers." Maggie stepped aside as Tom entered.

Connie had returned to her desk, but stared out the window at her view of the harbor.

"Good news, Connie," Tom whooped, striding into her office. "More fuel for Clarence Roberts' funeral pyre."

As Connie turned, Tom jerked to a standstill. Glazed, far-away eyes stared from the face of a woman he did not know. To his horror, nine crushed and dried bugs marched in a meticulous row along the perimeter of her desk.

"Don't write the last page, Tom," Connie whispered.

"What?"

"Don't write the last page. The world ends when you do." Connie's garbled, rambling speech was almost unintelligible.

"What the hell? Connie, you make no sense. Maggie is beside herself. What's wrong with you?"

Connie ambled across the room and clasped the lapels of Tom's jacket. "The cat's in the cradle," she rasped. "The cat's in the cradle."

Tom knew Connie needed help. More help than her staff could give her. Psychological problems plagued his oldest sister, Lindsay. She used the same slurred, meaningless speech when she suffered a psychotic breakdown.

"Sit, Connie. Sit here at your desk. Let me go get help." Tom took her arm and steered her toward the desk chair.

"I don't need help. The cat's in the cradle." Connie protested, but allowed Tom to guide her across the room.

After seating Connie, Tom returned to Maggie. "You're right, Mags. She's saying some strange things. And she's acting like a robot."

"What can we do?" Maggie's face reflected both horror and concern.

"Get help, that's for sure. We can't handle this alone. Call Robin Benson. He's her friend, but he's also a priest. He'll think of something. I'll go back and stay with her. Let me know when you get through to him."

Robin was leaving his office when the phone rang. He almost didn't answer. He needed to visit sick parishioners at the hospital. A sixth sense told him the call concerned Connie. He had worried about her all morning.

When Robin answered, Maggie's panicky voice echoed through the receiver. "What shall we do, Father Benson? Connie's out of her mind. She needs help."

Robin's voice remained calm, but his mind raced. Connie needed professional help, more than he could give. "Let me call Bob Coble," he told Maggie. "He's one of my parishioners and I think he's Connie's doctor. I'll get back to you as soon as I know anything. In the meantime, stay with her and don't let her leave the office."

Dr. Coble didn't like interruptions during office hours. But when told Father Robin Benson called with a crisis, he hurried to the telephone.

"Sounds like she's experiencing some sort of psychotic breakdown, Robin," Dr. Coble said. "Take her to the emergency room immediately. I'll alert them you're coming. I'm tied up right now but the E. R. doc can handle it. I'll check on her later."

"Do you think so? She seems rational at times. Then she'll say or do something totally bizarre."

"I think she needs to be checked out. She may resist. She probably thinks she's fine. But bring her. Don't let her drive herself."

Robin telephoned Maggie with the doctor's instructions. "Dr. Coble wants her brought to the hospital. Get her ready and ask Tom Crouton if he'll go with me."

"That's ridiculous!" Connie sputtered when Robin arrived. "I'm not going to any hospital. I'm working. We've scheduled a property appraisal this afternoon."

"You *are* going, Connie. Dr. Coble insists. Here. Take your pocketbook. "Robin was frustrated and didn't want to hold a woman's purse. This one sported a shoulder strap. He tried arranging it on her arm, but it dragged the floor. When he stretched the strap over her head, she pulled away. Finally, he looped it over his own shoulder. It banged against his hip as they struggled.

"Grab an arm, Tom," Robin gasped. "That way we can work our way toward the door."

Connie dug her feet into the carpet like a stubborn child. "I'm fine, I tell you. Leave me alone so I can get back to work."

The men inched Connie out of her office and into the hall. As she left, she glanced at Maggie, mistaking the concern on her face for amusement.

"Oh, now I get it. You guys are playing a joke on me." Connie laughed in relief. "Okay. I can go along with that."

The hospital staff expected them, having been briefed by Dr. Coble. Dosher Hospital in Southport was old, but well equipped. A small, state-of-the art psychiatric ward occupied the third floor. The doctor considered sending Connie to the larger and newer hospital in Wilmington, but she needed immediate care. And the Dosher staff excelled in treatment of distraught patients.

"I'll stay with her, Tom," Robin said when they arrived. "You probably need to get back to work."

Tom left gladly. The whole scene brought out skeletons from his family closet. More than once he had chafed under the impersonal glare of an emergency room light when admitting Lindsay to the psychiatric ward.

"Bring her to the examining room." A nurse greeted them and replaced Tom at Connie's right arm. "Come this way, Father Benson. My name's Mary. I'm the nurse in charge today. Dr. Coble phoned, so we've been expecting you."

Connie fought as she was propelled through the outer office. "Leave me alone. Let me get back to work. I know this is a joke. I know you're all playing a joke on me."

"Keep her in here, Father Benson. I need to get some paperwork." Mary left Robin and Connie alone in the tiny cubicle. Sterile, cold, antiseptic, the room gave Robin the impression of belonging to a hospital of the future, one manned by robots and machines rather than people.

Connie sat briefly on the hospital cot, then jumped up and began pacing. She circled the room, stopping at each object she encountered. She picked it up everything and examined it. A box of Kleenex, a tongue depressor, an otoscope, all received minute scrutiny. Then she carried her treasure to her next stop and hid it—in a trashcan, behind a chair, under her pocketbook.

"Connie, please sit down," begged Robin. "The doctor will be here in a minute."

Connie studied his face. *Oh that's Robin,* she thought. *He's party to the joke. Party. That's it. They're keeping me here while they plan a surprise party. Maybe it's at the office. Or maybe right here in the hospital. I'll bet everyone is congregating downstairs. Soon they'll take me there and we'll have a wonderful time.*

She crossed the room and hugged Robin. How comfortable he felt. How secure. Somewhere in her confused mind she realized he anchored her stormy emotions.

Soon she resumed her ritual of circling the room and examining what she found. At intervals she returned and clung to Robin. He no longer tried to reason with her, she seemed harmless. But he wished the doctor would hurry.

Mary returned with a clipboard. "Miss Edmonds, please sign this."

"What is it? I'm not signing anything."

"We need your signature—so we can help you."

"No. I don't want help." Connie slammed the box of cotton swabs she held against a metal table. Little jars and vials teetered wildly, precariously close to crashing to the floor. "Quit treating me like a baby, ordering my every move. I'm an adult I tell you. An adult. You all are playing a joke on me." Connie threw the swabs against the wall and flew into Robin's protective arms.

"Please Connie," Robin begged, stroking her shiny auburn hair. "You do need help. Please sign the papers."

"No. Don't ask that of me. Robin, don't make me sign my name."

The nurse eased the clipboard in front of Connie. She had done this before. "Miss Edmonds, just mark an X on this line. We won't insist that you sign anything. But this will let the doctor examine you."

"I won't agree to a pelvic exam."

"No pelvic. I promise." Mary's voice sounded calm, reassuring. Maybe she could be trusted.

Reluctantly, Connie took the pen. Robin steadied her arm as she made a shaky X across the length of the page.

Mary took the clipboard, patted Connie's shoulder, then drew back the curtain, signaling the emergency room physician to enter the cubicle. The doctor entered abruptly. He acknowledged Robin, then began a cursory examination. "Give her 10 milligrams of Valium, Mary," he ordered.

"That should calm you, Miss Edmonds," he mumbled as he hurried from the room.

Robin turned to follow but Connie stopped him. "Don't go, Robin. Oh please don't go."

"I'll go, Father Benson," Mary said. "I'll find out what the doctor plans and let you know." Mary gave Connie a shot, then left them alone.

Connie became calmer. She stopped the horrible pacing and sat quietly on the cot. Only her hands revealed her agitation. Her fingers twitched and intertwined with a life of their own.

At length Mary returned with a wheelchair. "I'm taking you upstairs, Miss Edmonds." Turning to Robin, she continued. "We're admitting her for observation. We really won't know much until tomorrow."

The Valium had dulled Connie's senses to the point of lethargy. Like a nearsighted woman hunting for her glasses, Connie eased herself into the chair. For safety's sake, the nurse secured her arms and legs with leather straps.

Connie spoke little on the long trip down the corridor. When she did, she used that slurred, faraway speech. Occasionally, she parroted one of her strange comments—"The cat's in the cradle," or "Don't let the ship sink." Otherwise, she languished against the confines of the chair. Robin didn't know which he preferred—the wild Connie or this dazed inert creature. He realized though her body rested, her troubled mind still hallucinated.

Mary wheeled her patient into an elevator but signaled Robin to stop. "This is as far as you go, Father Benson. You may check on her tomorrow."

Connie stared at Robin through glazed eyes, her body slumped against the taunt straps that restrained her. *I know that man,* she thought. *I know him, but I just can't place him.*

Robin's last impression of Connie recalled an old horror movie he'd once seen, about a lunatic being wheeled into an insane asylum.

"And who is this, Mary?" A bright, chirpy redhead met them as they left the elevator.

"This is Connie Edmonds, Suzy. The doctor wants her in isolation tonight, for observation. She's had a rough day. I've given her a sedative and she's calmer now. If she does all right, move her to the floor tomorrow."

"Well, let's get you out of that chariot, Sweetie." Mary and Suzy hoisted Connie to her feet. With their support she shuffled into a tiny room, furnished with a single, utilitarian-looking iron bed. At the door, a small observation window provided the one break in an otherwise drab green interior. To Connie, the room looked like a prison cell.

After Suzy closed the door, Connie heard the clank as a lock turned, then dropped into place. She plopped on the bed. Robin had gone—somewhere. Shivering, she drew the single bed sheet around her shoulders. Wherever she was, she was really cold.

At length she stood and paced her confines. Looking through the small window, she saw an empty hallway. Oh yes. Now she remembered. *Everyone was downstairs, planning her party.*

Again she paced the room. *Nothing there. But faces at the window. Her demon, with a smile on her face. Talking to Lucy. Okay. They were probably checking on her so she wouldn't come out and spoil the surprise.*

Resume pacing. *A nurse at the window. Suzy, she was called. Would she come to the party?*

Suzy gone. Who was that? A clown. A clown wearing a red and green wig with a big red nose. Connie giggled. *Of course. You need a clown at a party. Sergeant Boggs. It was Sergeant Boggs dressed as a clown. She hadn't seen her in years.*

Suzy again. Then Amanda. With her father. And Sergeant Boggs—laughing and joking like the best of friends. But Amanda was dead. Oh well. She probably came back for the party.

Connie sat on the bed, watching the parade of faces at her window. They all appeared happy, waving to her and shouting, "Be patient. We're almost ready."

Finally she curled up in the bed sheet and lay down. The Valium quieted the demons and she rested. But she wished the party would start. *It was really cold in here.*

Chapter 12

Incarceration

"Connie ...?" Robin stepped tentatively into the hospital room, a sheaf of flowers in his hand.

"Come in, Robin." Connie turned in the bed and focused her eyes on a digital clock. Noon. She had slept most of the morning. During the night Suzy the nurse had given her a pill then wheeled her from isolation into a private room, or was that this morning? She couldn't remember.

"Connie? H-How are you?" Robin eased toward the bed. His hand shook as he reached out to touch her blanket. The floor nurses had told him she'd regained her senses. But after the trauma of last night, he had to see for himself.

"I'm fine, Robin. Just really, really tired. What's the matter? Why are you so upset?" He had lowered his head and buried his face in his arm. Connie heard one giant sob.

"I was just so worried. We all were." Strangely, the normally shy man didn't mind letting her see him cry. *He has a tender heart,* thought Connie.

Robin wiped his eyes and searched for a place to deposit the flowers. Seeing none, he shrugged his shoulders and laid them on a counter.

"Well, that's ridiculous. I guess I got a little over-excited or something. But why did you bring me to the hospital? I could have straightened myself out at home." Connie slowly recalled images of the morning and night. Embarrassed, she chided herself for acting so strangely. *Not very professional,* she thought.

"Connie, you weren't all right. We were scared to death," he repeated. Finding Connie in her right mind delighted Robin. A goofy, schoolboy grin plastered itself on his face and remained there for the rest of his visit. It had been years since anyone close to him had caused this much worry.

Connie noticed the happiness in his face. But the whole situation puzzled her. "Robin," she whispered. "I think I'm on the psychiatric ward. This place is weird. I don't have a telephone. And they told me I couldn't go off the floor. I can see the elevator from my bed. Everyone punches in some sort of secret code before they get on. And this woman next door. She's either screaming or moaning all the time. I heard one of the nurses say something about shock treatment for her. Am I on the psyche floor, Robin? Am I?"

Before Robin could answer, a huge shadow blocked the light from the hall and fell across the floor. A gigantic man appeared in the doorway. Curly black hair set off a merry smile and kind gray eyes. Huge shoulders looked like they could carry the weight of the world.

The giant shambled into the room with a rolling, Grizzly bear gait. "Morning folks. Top of the morning to you. I'm Wayne. Wayne Bailey. I'm your nurse this morning. Know I'm not as good looking as most nurses, but what can I say? An old boy raised in the hills of Tennessee needs brawn, not beauty."

"You're a nurse?" asked Robin. "I thought all nurses were women."

"Oh no. This women's liberation movement works both ways. Girls are wanting men's jobs. So why can't a man do a woman's job? Actually, I'm a CNA—Certified Nurses' Assistant, thanks to a crash course at the community college and some years with Uncle Sam. I assist the nurses in everything except giving medication. Funny. They usually need assisting when some big old fellow needs lifting off a bedpan."

When Wayne laughed, his belly shook like Santa Claus. The joy began in his eyes and coursed through his body. You could not be in the giant's presence without smiling. Connie and Robin found his good humor made the small joke funnier than it might otherwise have been.

"Miss Edmonds," he continued, "I do need for you to sign these forms. Mary got you to mark an X on them last night. That was okay temporarily. But we need your signed consent to keep you here."

"Well good." Connie sat straighter in bed. "I won't sign anything. I'm ready to go home."

The joy and kindness never left Wayne's eyes. But his body stiffened with the determination that had enabled him to brave enemy fire in Vietnam. "Miss Edmonds. Connie. Going home is not an option. You were one sick cookie when your friends brought you in last night. You're better now, but you're far from well. If you don't voluntarily admit yourself to Dosher, we will have no choice but to get a court order to commit you—to the state psychiatric hospital in Raleigh."

Connie and Robin gasped in unison. "Then I *am* on the psychiatric floor," she breathed.

"Yes Ma'am. You are. And I guarantee you'd rather be here than up in Raleigh."

With no further resistance, Connie reached for the papers. This time she carefully penned her signature at the bottom of a long, legalistic form.

"I'll be off the next few days," Wayne said. "But I'll be checking with you when I get back. You folks have a nice morning." Wayne touched his forehead in salute and ambled out the door.

After Wayne left, Robin crossed to Connie's bed and took her hand. "Nice man. I think you're in good hands. But I've neglected my duties too long. I've got to get back to work."

Connie's face fell. "Must you go, Robin? I hate being alone in this horrid place."

Robin caressed her cheek. She looked so helpless, like a little doll propped against a great white pillow, decorating a child's bed. "I'll come back tonight. The nurses gave me a list of what you'll need. Dilcey will help me find everything." He didn't mention that he had been warned not to bring anything with which patients might harm themselves and that the hospital staff would search Connie's belongings before they were given to her.

"Why are these lying on the counter? Nasty. Nasty. Doctor would never approve. So unsanitary." A thin, dried-up shrew in a white uniform bustled into the room and grabbed Robin's flowers. She held them over the wastebasket, ready to dispose of them.

"Don't throw those away," Connie cried. "My friend didn't know what to do with them. Can't you find a vase?"

The shrew regarded her over a beak-like nose. Connie noticed the skin drawn across her cheeks and brow. It was as crinkled and transparent as parchment. Salt and pepper gray hair was knotted into a tight bun on the crown of her head. Her badge identified her as Harriet Pringle, R.N. *Prickle is more like it,* thought Connie.

"Young lady, this is a hospital, not a florist. Doctor demands we be sanitary." Prickle left, however, and returned with the flowers in a lopsided plastic container. "This is all I could find. Can't have glass in here. We might hurt ourselves, you know. Now. Have we had our B. M. today?" As she spoke, Nurse Pringle reached for the chart attached to the foot of the bed.

"I beg your pardon?"

A slow, superior smirk inched across the dried-up face. "A B. M. Miss Edmonds. Bowel movement. Have we had our bowel movement today? Doctor says that healthy bowels mean healthy bodies."

"What business is that of yours?"

"No need to be offensive." Prickle seemed personally affronted. She scribbled in the chart and smirked again. "We will rest today. Tomorrow we must be up and about. We go to large group at nine. Doctor comes to see us at ten. In the afternoon we go to small group."

"No thanks. I'll just rest in my room."

"Oh, no, no, no. Doctor wants us to participate. That's how we get better."

Connie had reached her limit. She sat up in bed and glared at the nurse. "Who the hell is 'Doctor'? And why do 'we' give a shit?"

Prickle waggled her finger at Connie, then scribbled in the chart. Without another word she replaced it and prissed out with her best professional strut.

Connie retrieved the chart from the foot of her bed. Today's entry was scribbled in tight, old-fashioned handwriting. "Patient belligerent and uncooperative. No progress."

For Connie, the rest of the week was mundane and depressing. She was coerced to go to group therapy and to see the doctor. In group she positioned herself as far from the others as possible. She didn't want to catch anything from those crazies. The doctor was no help. Connie knew he was a psychiatrist. He would ask some stupid question and wait for her answer. Why didn't he fix her instead of sitting there like an idiot, waiting for her to reveal some deep, dark secret? She had little to say, so they sat in silence until her time was up.

By Friday night the confines of her situation finally closed in on her. Connie felt her life force ebb to its lowest. Why did she have to be locked up? What made the people who called themselves "professionals" think she was incapable of functioning? The screaming maniac next door needed to be here. But she didn't. She could take care of herself. Didn't she manage her own business? Wasn't she a respected member of Southport society?

The injustice of it all overwhelmed her and made her furious. Leaping from her bed she began screaming. "Damn, damn, and damn!" she shouted, giving her bed a resounding kick. Grabbing the first thing available, she hurled Robin's flowers against the wall. Water and stems spewed across the room. In the process, she got soaked. "Damn!" she repeated, giving the bed another kick.

"Hey, hey, hey. What's going on, Sunshine?" The huge arms of Wayne Bailey engulfed Connie. In the doorway she saw two orderlies, their eyes widened in amazement.

Freak, she thought. *They think I'm a freak. I'm locked up here in the loony bin for everyone to stare at.* Since she couldn't break Wayne's grasp, she beat his chest in frustration. "Let me go, you big ox. Let me go!"

To Connie's utter amazement, Wayne burst out laughing. His grip loosened but still she couldn't break free. "Sunshine, you take the cake. They told me you were having another breakdown. You're just pissed off. I've been around enough to know the difference between a psychotic woman and a mad one."

"You're damn right, I'm pissed! And one thing that really pisses me off is you calling me 'Sunshine!' What's that supposed to mean?" Connie gave his chest another whack. She realized she was screaming. She didn't care. It felt good to spend the excess energy she'd stored during a week of confinement.

Again Wayne laughed his deep belly buster. He relaxed his hold and steered Connie to the comfortable visitor's chair. "Sit here. You're all wet. I'll get your robe. I guess you didn't know you're called 'Sunshine' on this floor."

"Sunshine?"

"Yep. Because you're always so grumpy. You've got quite a reputation among the staff, Ma'am."

"I'm sure Nurse Prickle thought that one up. She's driving me crazy coming in every night screeching, 'B. M.? B. M.?' I'd like to B. M. her. Now do what Nurse Pringle would do—go write bad things about me in my chart."

"I'm not going anywhere. I'm going to sit here with you while you dry off, calm down, and tell me what's so wrong."

Wayne brought a towel and began to rub Connie's hair. She felt like a puppy that'd been given a bath and was being dried by its master. For such a big man, he was surprisingly gentle. His hands did more than dry her hair. They soothed her soul. She felt her head and neck, then her entire body, relax.

They didn't talk for at least five minutes. Wayne continued rubbing Connie's hair, then massaged her shoulders. She slipped into a kind of trance. When he did speak, it was with the kindest voice she had ever heard.

"So what's wrong, Sunshine? You're obviously miserable. Your chart shows you've made no progress." Wayne had ended his massage and sat beside her.

Connie rested her head on the back of the chair. She was warm and comfortable, more content than she'd been in weeks. "Oh, Wayne. It's awful here. Just awful. Nurse Prickle is bad enough. But I'm stuck here with a bunch of maniacs. I can't even shave my legs without someone watching to see I don't do myself in with the razor. I've got a life. I've got a business. Things are happening on the outside that I need to direct. I have responsibilities. I want out of here."

"The outside can wait, Connie. As far as this floor, there are no maniacs here." Wayne's voice had lost the gentleness, but none of the kindness. "There are people here who are tired, or confused, like you, or battling some sort of addiction. But no maniacs. The lady next to you lost her husband and son in the same automobile accident. She sees no reason to go on living. But she cooperates. She works with us as we try to help her."

"How tragic. But I've had no trauma like that in my life. I guess I *was* confused, earlier, at my office and when I came to the hospital. But I'm all right now. Why can't I go home?"

"Because you don't cooperate. You go to group and sit there like a bump on a log. You won't talk to the psychiatrist. Sure, you could go home. Probably function for a while. But I guarantee you'd be back here in a few months."

"Is that what it takes to get out of here, cooperation?"

"Among other things. We give you skills to cope in the outside world. Right now you're too vulnerable. You have no understanding of your psyche. You need to look at what caused you to land here in the first place. And what to do if it happens again."

They continued to sit in silence. At some point, Wayne had taken Connie's hand. It rested there, like a leaf in a bear's paw. Wayne squeezed her hand and asked gently, "Is there more, Sunshine? Is there more than being miserable because you're here?"

"Well, I suppose I feel pressure from my business. We had a terrible disappointment recently, a project we've worked on for several years has fallen through."

"Why?"

"What do you mean, why?"

"Why did the project fall through? You don't strike me as a woman who lets much stand in her way. And you're the most successful developer in Southport. I may be new to the area, but I see your face and name plastered on billboards and 'For Sale' signs all over town."

Connie had not intended to reveal herself to anyone at the hospital. They couldn't force her out of her shell. But it was so easy to talk to Wayne. She found that as she talked, her burden lightened. She told him about the apparent failure of Turtle Nest and the harassment of Clarence Roberts.

"Why does Senator Roberts hate you so?" Wayne's perceptive mind had focused on the problem.

"Because of something that happened long ago. Please. I'd rather not talk about it."

"You need to. Don't you see? In hiding from us, you're hiding from yourself. Why does Clarence Roberts hate you?"

"Oh Wayne." She was becoming upset again. Her face and hands twitched in agitation. He knew he had to walk the fine line between confession and over-stimulation. "He blames me for his daughter's death, her suicide. Like I said, it was long ago."

"The important thing is, do you blame yourself? Outsiders really can't hurt us. Not like we can hurt ourselves."

Connie sat up straight. The relaxed mood was gone. She held her arms and shoulders rigidly, pressed taunt against the back of her chair. Her face contorted in anguish as little beads of sweat marched across her forehead.

Connie's mind replayed a scene acted out many years before. Wayne was silent, so she gave voice to what she saw. "I do, Wayne. Oh, I do. I killed her just as if I'd tied the sheet around her neck and kicked the chair away. To make matters worse, I lied. I lied and protected the scumbag sergeant who drove her to suicide."

Connie slumped in her chair. She'd never admitted it, to herself or anyone else. But it was true. She blamed herself for Amanda's death, and for the cover-up. Wayne must think her trash. "So now you know. Go scribble that in your chart. The psychiatrist will have a field day. And feel free to hate me. I deserve little more."

For the first time since she'd known him, the light left Wayne's eyes. He seemed to age ten years. His shoulders drooped as he ran his hand through his curly hair.

When he looked at her again, it was with infinite sadness. "Ah, Sunshine. I don't hate you. Never. How could I? But you need to hear my story. No one in Southport knows. But you must, for your own sanity. I've got to finish rounds tonight. I'm off at eight in the morning. I'll be back."

Wayne left then, walking like a tired old man rather than one in his prime.

Connie sat in her chair, rehashing the extraordinary events of the evening. When she got cold, she climbed back into bed. *Fool*, she thought. *You'll never see him again. He's probably at the nurses' station having a good laugh with those orderlies. Then he'll write in my chart, right below Nurse Prickle.*

Chapter 13

Vietnam Revisited

True to his word, Wayne entered her room at 8:30. Connie had convinced herself he wouldn't come. But she'd been furtively glancing at the door and clock. He said his shift ended at 8:00. If he didn't come by 9:00, she was putting him in the category with Nurse Prickle.

"Morning, Sunshine," Wayne teased. "Gosh, you look better when you're dry."

In spite of herself, Connie laughed. "I suppose so. I did throw quite a tantrum last night, didn't I?"

She was seated in the visitor's chair, finishing her breakfast. Wayne joined her, lowering himself into the only other seat in the room, a narrow, straight-backed contraption that creaked in torture beneath his huge frame. He had brought a pot of coffee and his own mug. He poured them both full cups of the steaming, dark brew, then set the pot on the small table between them.

"Thought I'd bring this along if we're going to pow-wow. Sorry it has to be decaf. I got permission from your doctor for you to miss the morning sessions. Pringle was not happy about that."

Connie groaned.

"Don't get me wrong," Wayne said. "Harriet Pringle is an excellent nurse. Just a bit overzealous."

They sipped their coffee in silence. Connie watched smoke rise from the steaming pot and evaporate into the room.

After an interval, Wayne set down his mug. "I promised to tell you my story, Sunshine."

"That's not necessary, Wayne. Let's forget last night. I'd like to." Connie laughed a nervous little laugh. She was embarrassed, partly because of her tantrum and partly because of her revelations about Amanda's death. In the light of day, it all seemed melodramatic. But last night was real. Too real.

Wayne looked at her evenly. He understood. He'd been in her shoes, denying, trying to forget. It didn't work.

"No, Sunshine. You're not getting off that easily. I'm here, missing my morning nap. You'll have to listen. I only ask one thing. Hear me out. Save your questions 'til the end. I've never told this to anyone, start to finish. I'm not sure I can get through it."

Connie shrugged. She didn't have anything better to do. At least she was missing that dumb group therapy thing. And his coffee was good.

"This tale begins twelve years ago, in 1965, when I was shipped to Vietnam. I was married and had finished two years of college at Lincoln Memorial University in Harrogate, Tennessee.

"I wanted to be a doctor so I had taken lots of courses in biology and chemistry. I planned to transfer to Knoxville to the university and finish my pre-med training. I even talked to the coach at Tennessee about walking on the football team. When he saw my size, he saw 'fullback' written all over me. Even mentioned a scholarship."

"So why'd you go to Vietnam? College boys weren't drafted."

"Please, Sunshine. No interruptions. Let me tell this my way. But to answer your question, you're right. I could have deferred since I was in college. But I had this crazy notion that I was a freeloader. Getting a cushy education while guys my own age were serving their country. I was twenty-one, and stupid. But idealistic. I've always been an idealist.

"At first, things were okay. They made me a medic, since I wanted to be a doctor and had taken biology. Medics were in short supply. They were getting blown up on the front every day.

"But I was pretty good. Surviving was simply a matter of finding out where the bullets came from. If a guy was going to get shot, it was usually in his first weeks in the field. He'd get scared or confused. Once you located the enemy, you went in the other direction.

"I learned to flatten this great bulk of mine against the ground and work my way to my wounded. The guys trusted me. They knew if they went down, I'd come get them.

"After six months in the field we could go to Hawaii for R and R—rest and relaxation. My wife met me there. We had a great time. We stayed a week. I was on top of the world. Six more months and I could become human again.

"When I returned to Vietnam, life wasn't boring, but it had a sameness to it. Get shot at. Rescue your men. Sleep in a tent, usually in the rain. Do it again tomorrow.

"Until one day when we were a little north of Da Nang. We weren't under fire, just walking through the bush. This little skinny kid, Huey was his name, from Cleveland, was in front of me. He wasn't a particularly good friend. Truthfully, I barely knew him.

"Huey was walking along, griping that his feet hurt. Then his legs and arms flew off in different directions. I swear. I never saw anything like it. He'd stepped on a land mine and gotten blown to bits.

"I stood there, stared at what was left of that poor sucker, and said, 'Damn. What a way to go.'

"I didn't think any more about it. Huey's death had been pretty spectacular. But I saw men die every day. Hundreds of them. What was one more bloke?

"It took several days, but we secured the area and were due to return to our base. My buddies and I were walking through this little village. The South Vietnamese lived like animals, whole families in one tiny hut.

"I looked in this one lean-to. All these slant eyes were clustered around a pot, eating their evening meal. They were laughing and jabbering away in what seemed to be ridiculous gibberish. Babies, toddlers, grandma and grandpa. There must have been fifteen of them.

"Why should they be in there enjoying themselves while poor Huey was blown up all over their landscape? We couldn't even find enough of him to put in a body bag.

"We knew the villagers cooperated with the enemy. Sure, they shouted 'American, American' when we walked by. But they were also informers for the Viet Cong.

"I snapped. I don't know why. I just lost it. Reaching into my vest I took out a grenade, pulled the pin, and threw it into the hut. Within seconds the place exploded. But not before I heard the screams of the adults who realized what was rolling across their dirt floor. To this day, I hear those screams."

Wayne had told this much of the story in a monotone, as if he were an observer rather than the key player. The coffee had long since grown cold. Now he leaned against his chair and closed his eyes. The pain on his face was obvious. Connie knew there was more.

When he spoke again, his voice broke with emotion. The wound was still raw. "Unfortunately, that's only part of it. I wasn't content to take the lives of those villagers. I had to come home and destroy my life, and my wife's.

"After I killed the villagers, I had a complete breakdown. I was sent to Saigon, then back to the States. I became a lunatic, out of control and a threat to myself and everyone I came in contact with.

"The Army didn't know what to do with me. I was overmedicated to keep me quiet. So overmedicated that I became addicted. They discharged me and said to come for check-ups at the veteran's hospital. All they did there was refill my prescriptions.

"I went back to Tennessee. Tried to resume my life—tried to work, tried to go to school. I couldn't function without the drugs. And I became an alcoholic. Finally, my wife left. Said she loved me but she'd had all she could take. I was either a raging maniac or a stoned zombie.

"I hit bottom. Became one of those homeless veterans you read about. I camped near the veteran's hospital in Johnston City. Had to be near my supply. I did odd jobs so I could buy booze. The Salvation Army fed me, but I was a bum.

"One day I was at the hospital for my weekly prescription. A new doctor saw me, Teddy Crenshaw. Fresh out of medical school, green as grass. He gave me a thorough physical. Spent an hour with me. Said he'd refill my prescription but that he was going to start reducing it. I panicked. Told him he was crazy. I couldn't live without my medicine.

"He said, 'Sure you can. And I'm going to help you. You and I are the same age. We speak the same language. From now on, every time you come here, I'll be your doctor.'

"To make a long story shorter, Teddy did help me. It took a long time—years. It was the hardest thing I've ever done. But he gradually weaned me off the drugs and liquor. And he listened to me. He was the first doctor who took the time to hear my story and didn't just try to patch me up with some drug.

"Teddy helped me get into the community college for my CNA training. He helped me get this job. I owe him my life. I'm going back to Tennessee, though. They've started a medical school at East Tennessee State University in Johnston City. I've been accepted as a first year medical student. I only hope I can be half the doctor Teddy Crenshaw is."

Wayne sat in silence, his story ended. The story had taken an emotional toll on both of them.

Finally, Wayne roused himself and patted her knee. "I have to be going, Sunshine. I've got to get some sleep since I'm on duty again tonight. Maybe my story will help you. Maybe listening to other peoples' stories will help. You feel responsible for one person's death. I caused the death of an entire family. But there's hope. I'm living proof that you can go on.

"The first thing you must do is get out of this hospital. The only way to do that is for the staff to see you're making progress. Go to group. Try to cooperate, even with Harriet Pringle.

"When you do get out, go see this woman." Wayne pulled a business card from his pocket. "Dr. Marty Connors, psychologist" was block lettered in bold black ink across the glossy white paper. "Teddy Crenshaw referred me to her. She's excellent. Tell her what you told me last night. Be completely honest. It will be the hardest thing you've ever done in your life, but it's the only way to heal."

Wayne stood and ruffled Connie's hair. "I don't leave Southport for another month. I'll be checking on you, Sunshine."

Chapter 14

▼

Psych Floor

Wayne visited her every day, even on his day off. He never mentioned her tantrum or his confessions. Scarred by his own life experiences, he survived by focusing on the future.

Today he found Connie sitting on the edge of her bed, applying makeup.

Because she couldn't have a mirror, her lipstick slid off the side of her bottom lip. Wayne took a tissue and cleaned her face. "So what do you think, Sunshine?" he asked.

"I hate it, Wayne. I go to group because you said it's the only way out of here."

"I'm getting glowing reports about you. Nurse Pringle is beside herself."

"Well, I force myself to cooperate," she said.

"That's okay, Connie. I learned long ago that you sometimes must act a part before you take it on."

"It seems I'm in therapy all the time," Connie moaned. "First there's large group with the hospital social worker, then I meet with a psychiatrist. After lunch there's small group. Any available professional leads that. I suppose you've conducted those sessions."

"I have. So has Nurse Pringle."

"Don't I know," grimaced Connie. "I was in her group yesterday. She had us gliding around the room, pretending we were birds." Putting down her lipstick she stood and extended her arms, flapping them in great, sweeping arcs. Pirouetting around the room, she mimicked the staid nurse. 'Doctor says looking at your problems from a distance helps put them in perspective,'" she croaked.

Wayne chuckled. "Connie, you do a perfect imitation of dear Harriet."

Tomorrow was Friday. She'd been here for over a week. Unbelievable. She'd lived a lifetime since then. Wayne and Nurse Pringle were people she would never have met in her old life. Robin came everyday. He had become such an important part of her life. Today she told him about Amanda's suicide. He deserved to know.

"So maybe that's what triggered this breakdown, Robin," she said. "That, and the flack I've gotten from Amanda's father over the years, and the high standards I put on myself at work. Lucy told me I needed counseling. Guess she was right."

Robin nodded. "Now I understand. I knew something was bothering you. There was sadness in your eyes that I never understood. I'm glad Wayne recommended a psychologist, and I'm glad you're going to see her."

Robin also filled her in with the work at the gravesite. "The media attention has died down a bit. That's because we're at what Dr. Beard calls "the boring stage of excavation." Right now his students are categorizing and labeling what they find. Doing the "grunt" work. But hopefully we can get some good press out of all of this. Burly Peters sent down a lady from the diocesan publicity staff. She spent the day showing our church secretary and me how to get positive media attention. We'll be sending out weekly press releases about progress at the dig. Maybe that will even generate contributions.

"How about Clarence Roberts," Connie asked. "What sort of noise has he been making?"

"Roberts has been strangely silent. Don't know if that's good or bad. I have heard through the gossip mill that he's been hospitalized. I believe he has lung cancer."

She'd told Robin that she wanted no visitors, except for him. Dilcey came anyway. "I just had to see you, Miss Edmonds. I had to see for myself that you were all right."

"I'm happy you came, Dilcey. It does get lonely up here."

Connie considered the petite black woman. Dilcey had worked for her for five years, but she knew little about her. Wayne had encouraged listening to other people's stories. She would start with her maid.

"Tell me about yourself, Dilcey. Tell me about your family. And why do you always wear violets pinned to your clothing?"

"Aw, Miss Edmonds. You don't want to know about me. I'm not very interesting." Dilcey took care of others. She didn't enjoy the spotlight.

"But I do, Dilcey. I really do. Why do you always wear flowers?"

"Well...." Dilcey lowered her face but looked up through her wire-rimmed glasses. "Well.... You might think it's childish, but they cheer me up. Sometimes I get sort of blue, scrubbing and cleaning and looking after my young'uns. But then I see these violets. They're my favorite. Remind me of all the lovely things God has made.

"I think that's why God put beautiful things on this earth, to help us mortals get through this life. That's what I call it, mortalizing—God sending us little messages that He's looking after us. When I get tired I remember He loves me just like He loves violets. Then I feel better. I always do. That's silly, isn't it?"

Deeply touched, Connie turned her head. She couldn't imagine spending her days cleaning people's toilets. And finding joy in the doing. "It's not silly, Dilcey. It's beautiful. Now tell me about your children."

This time, Dilcey showed no reluctance. Proud of her brood, she talked freely. "Well, I've got eight, you know. They're all smart and give me no trouble, except maybe for Ben, my oldest.

"Ben's had a hard time growing up, Miss Edmonds. He's been so lonely. He's real shy. Prefers his pets to other young'uns. But I think he's made some friends. He's been hanging around with some boys after school. I think he's feeling better about himself."

Dilcey stayed for thirty minutes. She entertained with stories of her children and Connie's cat. As she left, she patted her employer's arm. "Hurry home, Miss Edmonds. I miss you and so does Katie."

Wayne came by later with long-awaited news. "You can go home tomorrow, Sunshine."

"Hallelujah!" whooped Connie. "I'll be out of bed and gone by eight A.M."

"No. You must stay for morning group and one last visit with the psychiatrist. Then you may leave. Did you call Marty Connors like I told you?"

"I did. On faith I'd soon be flying this coop. I have an appointment next Wednesday."

"Don't be put off when you meet Marty. She's unique. She's also brilliant. And very intuitive."

Robin would pick her up at two o'clock. She couldn't wait. She missed her home, and Katie. Dilcey had said the cat was depressed. Connie would take care of that. "Extra Kitty Treats for you tonight, baby," she murmured.

Nurse Pringle bustled in to make a final entry in Connie's chart. "Doctor sent these instructions." She handed Connie a typed sheet titled *Hints on Resuming a Normal Life*. "He wants you to continue your medication and call if you have any problems."

"Nurse Pringle?" Connie paused until the woman looked up from her chart. "I had a B. M. this morning."

The nurse's face filled with happiness. "That's wonderful news, Miss Edmonds. Wonderful. Doctor says that means the system is opening up and things are flowing smoothly." She wrote in the chart with a flourish, then beamed at Connie before exiting with that mincing professional gait.

Connie didn't see her leave. Her hands covered her face, checking laughter that bubbled like lava from a live volcano.

Chapter 15

Dr. Marty Connors

Wayne had warned her. She thought she was prepared. But when Marty Connors answered her knock, Connie did a double take. She didn't know what she'd expected. A late-blooming hippie, maybe, or a dramatic sort. What she encountered was the loudest, brashest woman she'd met in years.

"Come in, Sweetheart. Come in." A multi-jeweled hand reached across the threshold and pulled Connie into the room. "Wayne called. I don't discuss my patients with other people. Didn't discuss you with Wayne. He just told me to be extra nice to you because you were one of his favorites."

Connie stood face-to-face with a woman who had wildly teased, bleached blonde hair, eyes coated green with eye shadow, and lips flaming red. Marty Connors looked more like an actress on opening night than a professional psychologist greeting her ten A. M. appointment.

Thick makeup made judging Marty's age impossible. Early sixties, probably. Ramrod tall, she carried herself with the regality of a queen. Some sort of caftan get-up draped across her shoulders and fell the length of her body. Her clothes hung like paisley sheets on a clothesline.

The psychologist worked out of her home. A sign in the front yard directed patients to the rear. While Connie had navigated the bumpy driveway, she compared the informal arrangement to the posh offices most doctors had.

The entrance opened through the kitchen. Before Connie arrived, Marty had been frying bacon—its piquant odor hung heavy in the air, grease pooled in the frying pan. *Strange,* thought Connie. *I would have expected a vegetarian.*

Marty steered her past the stove toward a narrow, dimly lit hallway.

"Right this way. Watch the dogs."

As Connie passed through the kitchen, two dogs stood and greeted her with friendly faces. With wagging tails they followed her, designating themselves as part of the therapy group.

To be kennel mates, they were a strange contrast. One was huge. A mutt, surely, but the recipient of many St. Bernard genes, its head the size of a full-grown pumpkin. The other was as tiny as its companion was large. A miniature Dachshund, it couldn't have weighed more than eight pounds. Connie could tell the dog was old. It looked at her through cloudy eyes. White hair tinged its muzzle and tail, otherwise, it was copper red.

The office was at the end of the hall. A deep sofa for patients stretched the length of the room. Connie sat on it, instinctively cuddling the teddy bear that had been propped against a pillow. Small dog struggled onto the cushions and nestled beside her. Big dog rested its great head in her lap, then burrowed in its doggie bed. Soon it snored softly. The animals were strangely comforting.

Marty fiddled with a tape recorder. "I hope you don't mind if I make tapes of our sessions. I may listen to them after you've gone. Often that helps me remember or get a new insight."

During the lull, Connie scanned the room. Modern artwork, an African folk mask, and a stuffed boar's head, decorated the walls. Just what she would expect, having met the psychologist. Over the desk was Marty's one tribute to conventionality. Two diplomas, a Masters from Duke and a Ph.D. from Emory, hung side by side. Prestigious schools. Maybe Marty did know her business.

"Now." Marty finished rummaging and settled into a chair. "Tell me your story. Start at the beginning."

"Well, Wayne said to tell you everything. But it seems foolish. Everything happened so long ago—over thirty years."

"The mind doesn't record time like we do, Connie," Marty said. "We bury hurtful memories, but our psyche holds onto old wounds and replays them like broken records. Just tell me what you remember, any detail. Something that seems unimportant to you may be the piece of the puzzle that we need."

"Well," Connie began. "I did have the breakdown, and Wayne helped me realize that I feel responsible for a young girl's suicide, and her father has persecuted me for thirty years, and I really need to get back to my business. We're planning a huge undertaking to promote our development property. And I have community responsibilities—I'm the chairwoman of—"

"Whoa," Marty pleaded. "You've given me a year's therapy material in your first sentence. Leave work and community alone. They will be there when you get back—those are other peoples' responsibilities now. Your job is to get well. Go back to what you told me at the beginning."

Connie outlined Amanda Roberts' suicide and Senator Roberts' harassment. She talked for an hour. The only thing she omitted, and she didn't know why, was her investigation of Roberts and the thick report Tom Crouton had compiled on him. For some reason, she clung to that information.

Marty never interrupted, not once. Occasionally she made a notation on a small pad. Mostly she listened. When Connie finished, Marty sat in silence, almost trancelike. Big dog snored—the only sound in the room. But Connie sensed a cumbersome burden lifted from her shoulders. She knew she'd been heard and believed this woman could help her.

Finally Marty spoke. "I must ask you, though I know the answer. Have you been tired lately, lost interest in things you normally enjoy?"

Connie rolled her eyes and nodded emphatically. "Have I ever."

"What you suffered is called an acute psychotic episode, with symptoms of depression. Your exhaustion is a symptom. You may never have an episode again, or you could have another next week. Our job is to minimize the likelihood of that happening.

"You've made a good start, coming here and being open and honest. Obviously, you've thought about this a great deal. I'm sure you realize your guilt feelings about Amanda's death comprise the root of your problem. Over the years, her father exacerbated this wound with his continued badgering.

"But the real culprit is you. You've spent the last thirty years burying this junk in your subconscious. You've tried overwork; you've strived for perfection. On some level, you believed if you led an exemplary life, you could erase the mistake you made when you were eighteen.

"You feel guilt over your role in the suicide. But you also feel guilty you're alive and Amanda's not. With every success, that little whiny voice of self-incrimination whispers, 'Sure, great for you, too bad Amanda Roberts wasn't so lucky. Better try harder to make amends.'

"Our subconscious mind is a powerful thing. Call it your spirit, God person, psyche, whatever—it's as much a part of you as an arm or a leg. I compare our subconscious to a giant kettle of soup. We put our life experiences in the pot and most of the time things simmer along pretty well. In your case, you tried to keep the lid on a brew that finally boiled over."

As Marty talked, Connie remembered her therapy on the psych floor. Do all humans experience these same basic needs? Acceptance and validity from the outside world, but also from one's own self? Something to think about.

"What about my hallucinations? What about all the weird things I said? What about my dreams? I'm such a practical person. They make no sense to me."

"Ah," Marty assured her. "That's where our work begins. That's how I can help you and how you can help yourself. I believe the images and hallucinations, all the strange things you said, meant you no harm. Actually, they strove for your good. I know they frightened you. But that's the way our subconscious speaks to us. It has no language, so must resort to images and symbols for attention. You've buried all this garbage from Amanda's suicide, from your days in the Army, whatever. Your psyche rebelled.

"I'm a follower of Carl Jung, a Swiss psychologist. Jung wrote about archetypes—symbols common to the human race. I can help you with these. But you must discover the significance of the visions. Since they're your images, only you can give them meaning."

"How long will all this take?"

"That I can't promise. You've spent thirty years getting into this pickle. It'll take a while to get you out. But we'll start now. As soon as you get home, jot down anything that comes to mind—thoughts about the suicide, your experience in the hospital—anything. And talk to people. Anyone who knows you may possess clues you haven't even considered.

"Keep a daily journal. Record not only your past, but also what you're thinking now. Each week we will discuss your findings, then outline a course of action. Things should fall into place pretty quickly, at that point. Can you do this?"

"I think so, Marty," Connie sighed. I'm not accustomed to thinking about myself. I've always been action-oriented, not introverted. But I'll try. See you next week."

As Connie showed herself out, big dog opened one eye and woofed a quiet good-bye.

Chapter 16

Revelations

"Connie, would you approve these plans for the party? I'm confirming my orders and checking final details." Janie Kilpatrick struggled into her office, burdened by several large bags and two newsprint tablets. Dropping these on the table she panted, "My committee and I made sketches. We want you to understand our vision of the layout. Everything must be perfect."

"I knew you were the right person for the job, Janie," Connie assured her. She had returned to work the week before and was surprised that her staff had functioned amazingly well without her.

"Of course, our color scheme is red, white and blue, since it's the Fourth of July. We'll display the Edmonds Company logo in prominent places—at the dock where the guests arrive, on the speaker's stand, that sort of thing. Since the purpose of the party is promotion of Turtle Nest, I thought we'd distribute turtle favors to everyone. Cute little rubber turtles they can put on their desks or take home for children or grandchildren. We'll pass out turtle pins for the ladies and turtle tie tacks for the men. Throughout the meal we'll draw names for door prizes like these …" Janie reached into one of her bags and produced a necktie decorated with turtles, a cap shaped like a turtle, and a tote bag with smiling turtle faces on the front.

"What fun, Janie. You're so creative." Connie donned the turtle cap and clowned in an ornate gold leaf mirror. "I've ordered sashes for all the staff in our navy blue company color. That will identify us if anyone needs help. May I see the sketches?"

Janie spread out a large sheet of newsprint. "This is our concept of logistics. You and Tom will stand at the dock, greeting guests as they arrive. Then it's a short walk to the refreshment tent. We'll serve cold drinks, tea, lemonade and some light wine or beer, along with a few hors d'oeuvres. Our guests will be hot from their trip across the inlet. But we don't want them overstuffed before we present our sales pitch.

"At the refreshment tent we'll have detailed drawings of our concept for the future of Turtle Nest. The staff will conduct golf cart tours of the island, pointing out highlights as they go. The adventurous can even climb Old Baldy for a look at the whole island.

"Around four o'clock we'll begin the program ... here." Janie pointed to one corner of the sketch. We'll stretch rows of picnic tables in front of the podium. Behind that, the inlet and a distant view of Southport will provide a scenic background for our speakers.

"As you suggested, I'll go first, welcoming everyone and detailing the program. Then Bill Pace will talk about plans for protecting the environment of Turtle Nest, as well as making it a sanctuary for the Loggerhead. Father Benson concludes with a brief history of the area and a description of the work going on at St. Bettina's."

"What are these penciled in drawings in this far corner?"

Janie giggled. "Those are the porta-potties. Don't laugh. Without those we'd have some pretty uncomfortable guests. And they're costing you a bundle."

"What about food?"

"After the program, the guests will move through the buffet line." Janie indicated its location on her sketchpad. "Betty Sue, the caterer, will prepare shrimp several different ways, plus chicken for those who don't want seafood. There's also corn-on-the-cob, baked beans, cole slaw, and hushpuppies, for side dishes."

"Janie, you've outdone yourself."

"And for dessert there's turtle cake. Throughout the meal Loggerhead Larry and the Turtle Shells will entertain us. Actually, it's Larry Logan from Holden Beach with his three-piece dance band. A platform for dancing will occupy center stage. We should finish about ten o'clock. That will give Captain Bob plenty of time to ferry everyone to the mainland. Then shuttles will take our guests to their hotels."

"Again, Janie, let me compliment you on a job well done. You could become a professional at this. But please, don't leave your day job."

"Just keep your checkbook open, Connie. All this isn't coming cheap."

After Janie left, Connie walked to her window and stared across the harbor. It felt good—being back at the office—comfortable. Marty Connors had told her to take it slow and she had, working half days at first. Now she welcomed this new challenge of a large-scale party.

Since her appointment with Marty, she had spent hours pondering the psychologist's words. Most of it made sense. But why hadn't she mentioned her investigation of Clarence Roberts? She didn't know. Maybe she would someday.

Connie had read about half of Tom Crouton's thick document on Clarence Roberts. If the rest proved as spicy, she could forever destroy Roberts' reputation. What should she do with the report? She hadn't decided. She could send a copy to the newspaper, the governor, or the senator himself. Or she could destroy it. Somewhere in her brain Revenge woke up and whispered, "Use it. You've suffered enough. Make him pay."

Maggie's page interrupted Connie's thoughts. "It's your mother on line three."

"Got it, Maggie. Thanks." Connie picked up the receiver and settled back in her chair. "Mom. What's up? How's merry old England?"

"Fine dear, fine. How are you?" Helen knew nothing of Connie's hospitalization yet she'd worried. Over the past few months, her mother's intuition had told her that Connie was not well. But she knew that Connie would never confide in her. Connie's pride saw to that.

"I'm okay. How about you and Dad?" On her part, Connie did not intend telling her mother she'd been sick. Helen would abandon her trip, fly home, and supervise the recovery.

"We're fine, dear. Couldn't be better. I wanted to tell you all that's happened. Got a minute?"

"For you, I've got lots of minutes. Tell on."

"Well, we had high tea with Madeline—the Duchess of Leicester. At least I did. Your dad dropped me off and went on to the Rat and Whistle." Helen giggled. "Your father's developed quite an affinity for English pubs.

"Anyway, Madeline and I had tea and dear little sandwiches and petit-fours, just like you read about in romance novels. While we were eating I told her about Suzanne Marshburn and her father, who had once lived in Madeline's home."

"I thought the duchess was a recluse."

"Oh dear me, no. We discussed that. She says the townspeople think because she's a duchess she won't associate with them. She's too shy to make the first move. But we got along famously. I'm taking her to market this afternoon. I'll introduce her around. And she's planning a trip to North Carolina in February, when it's really cold in England."

Connie groaned. She could imagine her mother descending on Southport, duchess in tow.

"Madeline knew that a sea captain once lived in the house. She'd found a trunk in the attic. It apparently had belonged to Suzanne's father as 'Captain William Anders Cogdill' was lettered on the top." Helen's voice became so shrill with excitement that Connie could hardly follow the conversation.

"Calm down, Mother. I can't understand you."

"So we opened the trunk. It was difficult, I'll tell you. The hinges had rusted so we had to pry them open with a steel bar. Finally, we forced them free. Inside we found old maps and charts, a telescope, several uniforms, and a plumed hat. We acted like two schoolgirls, reading old love letters and trying on the clothes. And," Helen paused for effect, "at the bottom, there were letters and a diary."

"Mother, what did they say? Did you read them?" Connie's voice rose in anticipation.

"Not then. It was too dusky in the attic and the writing was old and faded. We took them downstairs.

"The letters were written by Suzanne to her father and dated 1863 to 1864. Sifting through the letters is not my cup of tea. They're mostly household details about running the plantation. I thought I'd bundle them up and send them to you. You can look through them, if you'd like."

"Oh do, Mother, do!" Now that her awful depression had begun to lift, helping with the investigation intrigued Connie.

"What else, Mother? Did you read the diary?"

Knowing she had her daughter's full attention, Helen prolonged the tale, even though she was paying for a transatlantic call. "Well, it grew late, so I fixed some scrambled eggs and toast. The duchess likes her eggs just the way your father does, cooked with lots of milk so they're—"

"Mo-ther. Get to the point. What was in the diary? Did it mention his 1859 visit to Suzanne on her plantation?"

"Well—yes." Helen was clearly disappointed at her daughter's impatience. "He wrote about it in detail. His youngest son, George, accompanied him. At first, they had a wonderful time. Parties were given for them in Wilmington and Southport, and all along the Eastern seaboard. They went to one in Charleston that lasted a whole week. The captain met Suzanne's friend, Rose Greenhow—was quite captivated with her, really. She had that effect on men. That's what made her such a valuable spy for the—"

"You're wandering again, Mother. What about the time around John Marshburn's death?"

"After the initial excitement, Captain Cogdill began noticing some strange happenings. He observed that the Marshburn children were shy and withdrawn, not lively like normal toddlers. And he worried about Suzanne. Often he wouldn't see her for days—she would send word she wasn't feeling well. Captain Cogdill and his son were left to spend a great deal of time with John Marshburn. At first the captain simply disliked Marshburn. Soon dislike turned to hate. John was a loud, boorish clod who delighted in overeating, over-drinking and whoring."

"Mother. I didn't know you knew such words."

"I wasn't born yesterday, you know. Anyway, John would disappear to the slave quarters every evening after dinner, whether Suzanne was there or not. It was no secret he was seeking a young black girl to abuse. He even suggested that Suzanne's father and brother join him. They were repulsed. Captain Cogdill noticed that many slave children on the plantation obviously had a white parent."

"What a disgusting man."

"That's for sure. And you remember that Marshburn died while beating a slave? Evidentially that happened frequently. He had a whipping tree in the yard. He hoisted the slaves up with their arms over their head and lashed them with a whip, men and women alike."

"Ugh."

"Yes, that was terrible. But Captain Cogdill lost his reason one day when he found Suzanne crying in the dining room. She hadn't heard him enter. When he touched her shoulder and turned her to him, he was shocked. Suzanne's face was swollen and her eye blackened. And a large gash seared her forehead."

"Let me guess—Marshburn."

"Of course. Besides whipping his slaves, he also beat his wife and probably his children. Captain Cogdill became incensed. He was ready to shoot Marshburn on the spot. Suzanne's hysterics were all that stopped him. She screamed that her husband was an excellent marksman and would kill her father. Then she would have the burden of her father's death on her shoulders."

"Why didn't she leave Marshburn?"

"That's what her father asked. After he got over the initial hysteria of Suzanne's beating, he begged her to return to England with him. But she said Marshburn would follow and kill her and the children. Captain Cogdill knew Marshburn was that cruel. He told his daughter to give him time. He would think of something."

"Did he?"

"Not exactly. But the next day Ellie, one of the house slaves, approached him. As he walked in the woods pondering the situation, she hailed him from the shadows. Ellie knew about Marshburn's ill-treatment of his family and Cogdill's vow of protection for Suzanne and her children."

"How did Ellie know?"

"Cogdill asked her that. She simply said house slaves knew everything that happened in the big house. She suggested the captain visit Alethia."

"Nettie Mae's great-aunt?"

"That's right. Captain Cogdill becomes vague after that. I suppose he didn't want to incriminate himself or his daughter. But I believe Alethia gave him a potion, causing Marshburn's heart attack."

"So why did Suzanne feel guilty? Why did she write the note implying she had committed a terrible crime?"

"Again, I can only guess. Captain Cogdill's ship was repaired sooner than expected. The entry of May, 1859 notes that the ship is ready and must sail immediately, with the tide. Perhaps the captain didn't have the opportunity to poison Marshburn. Perhaps Suzanne carried out the actual deed. We may never know the answer to these questions. The next entry is dated October, 1859. Cogdill wrote that Marshburn was dead and that he wanted to bring Suzanne and her children to England.

"The rest of the diary chronicles the remainder of his life. Suzanne and the children could not join Captain Cogdill until the Civil War ended. Apparently, she then suffered a mental breakdown. Her father referred to her being insane and hospitalized at the York Hospital. After she was released, she lived with Captain Cogdill at the family home. He worried about his daughter's future. Because of her 'mental affliction', everyone except the local Anglican priest, a Reverend Thaddeus Hepplewhite, shunned her. At one point he hoped Suzanne would marry the priest, but she never did."

"Mother, what a sleuth you are. Is the mystery solved? Are you coming home?"

"I think we've learned all we can here about the Cogdills and the Marshburns. We leave day after tomorrow for Switzerland. Your father says he's always wanted to yodel. Madeline is coming with us."

As Connie replaced the receiver, she realized she was exhilarated, but exhausted. Strangely, Suzanne Marshburn's tribulations over a hundred years ago had drained her. Thank goodness tomorrow was Saturday.

Chapter 17

Lucy James

Connie's one plan for the weekend was to seek out Lucy James. Marty Connors insisted that part of her therapy consisted of talking to people who knew her well. Lucy remained her one link to her days in the WACS and to Amanda's death. And Lucy had broached the subject of her own problems that had been caused by the suicide. Shuddering, Connie remembered Lucy's hell, precipitated by the tragic death.

"Please come. Spend the night. And bring Katie." Lucy had been overjoyed when Connie had called.

That was how she found herself driving up highway 17, early Saturday morning, with a mad cat in her car. Katie hated travel. She considered confinement in a Kitty Karrier an insult to her feline dignity. She hissed and clawed at the cage until exhausted. Then she slept, but returned to peevishness whenever the car slowed.

"I wish I'd left you home," Connie fumed. "If you hadn't received a special invitation, that's what would've happened." Katie answered with a grating scratch on the bars of her carrier.

Truthfully, Connie appreciated the cat's company. She was sailing into uncharted waters and Katie served as a familiar landmark.

Connie had visited Lucy's home before, but only briefly. Lucy lived in New Bern, one of the oldest cities in North Carolina and the site of the colonial government during the Revolution. She and her new husband had bought a townhouse that had been built during that era. With extensive remodeling, they had turned it into a showplace.

Lucy greeted them at her front door. "Come in, come in. How's my precious kitty?" she asked, reaching for the cat. Katie purred and preened as if she'd spent the last two hours in perfect contentment instead of unbridled fury. Connie shot her a dirty look.

"Charlie's gone this weekend, so we have the house to ourselves. Your room is at the top of the stairs. Let me help you."

Lucy hoisted her bag and led them up the narrow staircase ascending from the foyer. At the landing, she pushed open the door to an elegant bedroom. A mahogany tester bed functioned as the focal point of the room. Its net canopy soared like a great white bird above its four posts.

Connie realized she was standing on a priceless Persian rug. "The room's like you, Luce," she complimented. "Beautiful."

Lucy hugged her. "I'm so glad you're here. Come down when you're ready."

For the first time in months, Connie relaxed totally. She and Lucy spent the weekend giggling. The silliest thing would set them laughing "Do you remember the night you came in drunk, Lucy? The first night we were in the WACS? I was sure you were a 'fallen woman.'"

"Well, I pegged you for the biggest prude in the state," Lucy rejoined.

There was serious talk as well. Connie told Lucy about her hospital stay. She had dreaded that. Now she realized how brave her friend had been in describing her own comedown and therapy—all caused by the trauma of Amanda's suicide. Lucy had warned her, but she had brushed the warning aside.

Connie should have known better than to worry. Never one to gloat, Lucy's sympathy was heartfelt. "I understand, Connie. I do understand. I'm just so glad you're getting help. Marty Connors sounds like a jewel."

"She is. And she's encouraging me to talk to everyone who knows me well. So, here goes. Do you have any answers, Luce? What helps you? How do you cope? We can't bring Amanda back. But driving ourselves crazy isn't the solution, either."

"Well," Lucy began, "I'm still in therapy. Probably will be for the rest of my life, though I don't go as often as I once did. And Charlie's precious. He knows about my past and loves me anyway. He's the balance in my life.

"Stay with Marty Connors, use her as a support system. Listen to everything she says. Sometimes I think my therapist comes up with some strange ideas, but he's usually right in the end.

"As far as bringing Amanda back, you're right. We can't. But we can make amends in other ways. The suicide has extended me, made me look beyond myself. I find consolation in doing for others, in my 'causes,' as you call them. In some strange way, this gives Amanda's death meaning. Sort of like it counts for something.

"One of my projects now is the shelter for abused women and children here in New Bern. I have a special understanding for the victims since I was one myself."

"Would that work for me?" Connie asked. "To have a 'cause?' To find someone who needs a helping hand?"

"It couldn't hurt. But don't think you'll ever completely forget Amanda's death. We're human. That would be asking too much."

They were sitting on a glassed-in porch. Charlie James was quite the horticulturist. His exotic plants made the room seem more like a jungle than a patio in downtown New Bern. Lucy rested under a giant banana tree, its huge, emerald green leaves partially blocking her face. Katie slept curled in a ball in her hostess' lap.

"I hear you're dating Robin Benson." Lucy changed the subject abruptly. As usual, she was brash and straightforward.

Caught off guard, Connie hedged. "Ah, well. I suppose you could say that. But how did you hear that, way up here in New Bern?"

"News travels fast in an Episcopal diocese. Especially when an eligible priest and beautiful woman are involved. Are you going to marry him?"

"Lu-cy." Connie's fingers twitched in exasperation. Nervously, she plucked at her sweater. She'd admitted to herself that she loved Robin. But she'd made no decisions beyond that.

"Has he asked you? Have you considered it?"

"No, he hasn't asked me. And of course, I've thought about it."

"Do you spend lots of time together?" Lucy pushed.

"Several evenings a week. And one date on the weekend. We don't stay out late on Saturday night since he has church the next day."

"Sounds serious to me. Are you sleeping with him?"

"Lu-cy," Connie repeated.

"Okay, okay. Maybe that's a bit too personal. Have you been to church with him? Heard him preach?"

"Well, no. He's invited me several times. But, I don't know. I just haven't gone."

"Hm-m-m, interesting." Lucy was momentarily silent. Then she continued. "I think you're afraid."

"Who, me?" Lucy had her full attention.

"I know, I know. You're forty-nine years old. You're a big, successful businesswoman—handle millions of dollars and all that. But you're terrified, Connie Edmonds."

"Me? Terrified? Of what?"

"Oh, I don't know. Several things, probably. Commitment, for one. Losing your independence. Maybe even Robin himself. People react in different ways to clergy. Some put them on a pedestal. Others are terrified of them. In a way, marrying a priest would be like marrying God. That's a heavy burden to carry."

Connie rubbed her brow as she considered her friend's words. She and Robin had never talked of marriage. But she had thought about it.

Lucy pressed on. "The independence thing is unimportant, nowadays. Clergy wives have careers, often with larger salaries than their husbands. The days of being required to teach Sunday school or sing in the choir are over. But the other, the fear of clergy, you should think about that."

"Why would I be afraid of a clergyman?"

"You said yourself you've never attended his church. Maybe that's all part of your guilt over Amanda's death. You can't forgive yourself, so you wonder, how could God, or his servant Robin, forgive you?

"But seems to me you'd want to hear him preach," Lucy continued. "He's eloquent in the pulpit. And your mother told me you were raised an Episcopalian. So it couldn't be unfamiliarity with the service.

"Think about it, Connie. Charlie James is the anchor that keeps my ship from floating away. Robin Benson might be yours."

Chapter 18

Bitter Enemies

On Monday Connie returned to her office, rested and refreshed. She and Lucy'd had fun, but they'd done some serious talking, too.

Throughout the morning she found herself replaying the conversation concerning Robin Benson. Her work suffered as she stopped at regular intervals, pondering Lucy's words. Should she take Lucy's advice and let the relationship move to a more serious level? Robin had given hints that he was ready for such a change. Around noon, she grew tired of her thoughts and announced she was going to lunch.

"That's odd," Maggie informed the others after Connie left. "She never breaks for lunch. Something's on her mind. Hope she's not going bonkers again."

Connie thought the fresh air might clear her head. Even though her private life was in limbo, she couldn't let it affect her business. That was a sure formula for going broke.

As she stepped from the security of her building she became aware of a shadow figure, a man, at her elbow. Glancing sideways, the impeccable suit and smooth-shaven, but cold, face of Joshua Dunn loomed into view. She hadn't seen him for months, since he hadn't attended the last restoration meeting.

"Mr. Dunn." Connie stopped abruptly, her shoulder colliding against his chest. She felt the lean, solid muscles of his torso, inhaled cologne of a vague, musky odor. Strangely, she thought of a jungle animal out for its nightly kill.

"Come with me," Dunn barked, grasping her arm and guiding her the ten feet to a table at a sidewalk cafe. "Can I order you something?"

"I beg your pardon?"

"You heard me. I assume you were going to lunch. I'm trying to be nice, so order something. What do you want?"

"I want to know why you accosted me just now. After that, you can explain why you sabotage our board meetings."

"Ah. So Pauline's been talking. Never trust a fat woman, I always say. But since you brought up Senator Roberts, and since you're not eating, I'll tell you why I'm here."

"Please." Connie regained her composure but anger kept her on guard.

"The reason I wasn't at the last board meeting was because Senator Roberts sent for me."

"And of course, when His Majesty the senator speaks, you jump," Connie said sarcastically.

"Shut up with your smart-ass comments. I'm here at the senator's request. Spending time with a bitch like you is not my idea of fun."

"Trust me, the feeling's mutual."

Dunn shot her a hate-filled glare, but continued. "Roberts is calling a truce. He wants the two of you to coexist. If not as friends, at least not as enemies."

"Why?"

"Roberts is dying, Connie. He has lung cancer. His years of smoking caught up with him. Funny, being a senator from North Carolina, he's always championed the tobacco industry. Now tobacco is killing him. He has only a few months to live. He wants to make the most of them."

"Which means ..."

"Okay. Here's the deal. Roberts will get off your back. He'll remove his opposition to Turtle Nest and the excavation at St. Bettina's. But he's asking for something in return."

"I'm sure."

"You tell the truth about Amanda's death, especially about LuElla Boggs' harsh treatment of her. He wants you to testify before the United States Congress."

"The man never ceases to amaze me."

"Senator Roberts hopes to leave a legacy. The Clarence Roberts' Armed Services Reform Law. He'll be remembered as the senator who proposed federal legislation against berating, harassing, or mistreating an enlisted man or woman. Roberts believes your testimony and the sad story of Amanda's death will sway

Congress toward a 'yes' vote. He might even win a Nobel Peace Prize if this concept spreads worldwide.

"If you help him, Senator Roberts will never bother you again. He even suggested he might even steer business your way, in the form of wealthy clients and favorable state contracts."

Ah ha, thought Connie. *Even approaching death has not changed Roberts. He continues putting himself first and manipulating others for his own gain.*

She had not decided whether to use the report on Roberts. Instantly, she made up her mind.

Dunn's rude behavior had focused her mind's eye on years of torment and humiliation at the hands of Clarence Roberts. Enough was enough. Marty Connors would advise against public exposure of the document condemning the senator, but she had other plans.

Facing Dunn head on she hissed, "This is my answer for your boss. Tell him I intend to destroy him. And I have the means to do so. For thirty years I've been at the mercy of that man. I've built my business in spite of his opposition. But I've learned from him. I've learned how to be cruel and spiteful to get ahead."

"Wha ...?" Dunn mumbled. Connie's barrage caught him off guard. He had expected gratitude for the offer—imagined himself a sort of fairy godfather, bringing good news to the humble. Now he was confused and at a loss for words.

Years of pent-up frustration made Connie spit out her final words at Dunn. Other diners stared as the angry woman jumped up and banged her fist on the table.

"Roberts will stop harassing me. He'll stop because he'll be the laughing stock of the country. He may even be brought up on criminal charges.

"Ask your master to remember all his sexual encounters. Not the cutesy ones whispered about in society columns—the more lurid ones—the ones he hid. Ask him about the son he refuses to acknowledge. Tell him not to worry if he can't remember details. He can read about them in the newspaper."

Chapter 19

Dilcey and Ben

Edmonds' Land Development was in an uproar. Plans for the party at Turtle Nest were in full swing. Connie felt like a fifth wheel. "I delegated too well," she whined. "You guys don't need me." Secretly, she was pleased with her efficient staff. They left her time to pursue her own life instead of needing to supervise.

Like today. It was a fine, late June day. She decided to go home early and take her small dory out on the waterway. Maybe she could snag a few crabs for supper. She hadn't done that since she'd been sick. Time to get back to normal.

As she pulled into her driveway, she noticed the garbage still in the bin. That's weird, she thought. Wasn't today garbage day? Dilcey should have taken care of that long ago.

Climbing the stairs to the main floor, she saw more evidence of chaos. The mop leaned dry and unused against the backdoor. The steps hadn't been swept. Mud tracked in on Monday was still clumped in piles on several steps.

What was going on? This was not like Dilcey. Normally she was through with her work and going home by the time Connie arrived. Pushing open the door, she heard strange, muffled noises. Did Katie have a hairball? Was the television on?

Connie stood in the doorway, searching for the source of the sound. It took her some moments to realize she heard sobs—quiet, desperate, heartbroken sobs. Dilcey sat slumped over the kitchen table, head in hands, shoulders heaving. She looked and sounded like a human who had lost all hope.

"Dilcey," Connie cried. "What are you doing?"

When Connie called her name, Dilcey started and almost fell from her chair.

"I'm so sorry, Miss Edmonds. I'm so sorry. I know the house is a mess. I'm so ..." Whatever else the woman was going to say was drowned in a torrent of tears.

Instinctively Connie rushed across the room and gathered Dilcey in her arms. "What's upset you so? The house doesn't matter. Just please tell me why you're crying."

"Nothing you can fix, Miss Edmonds. Nothing anybody can fix. I best be going. I'm sorry about the house. I'll come back tomorrow and do my work." Dilcey pulled away and started for the door. Connie knew she would never make it to the bus stop.

"Dilcey Reynolds, you come back here. You come sit down and tell me exactly why you're bawling your eyes out." Connie amazed herself with her sternness.

Like a lost child, Dilcey did as she was told. She sat at the kitchen table sniffing and trying to control her emotions. Connie brought Kleenex. It took six tissues for Dilcey to calm herself enough to talk.

"Oh Miss Edmonds. It's my boy Ben. He's in jail!" The floodgates opened and tears again gushed forth.

"Stop it, Dilcey. I can't understand what you're saying, something about Ben. If Ben's in trouble we can't help him with you sitting here blubbering."

Surprisingly, the tears dried instantly. Always practical, Dilcey realized the truth in Connie's words. "That's true, Miss Connie," she said. "That's true."

Connie noticed the use of her first name. That was a first. Connie knew it indicated a subtle shift in Dilcey's regard for her. Something to do with trust and friendship. She realized that she, too, had come to regard Dilcey as a close friend.

"Good. Now tell me what happened."

"Like I said, Ben's in jail. He was arrested last night. I was down there most of the night and early this morning. Chief McLeod say he were vanzadizing."

"Vandalizing?"

"Yes'm. Vanzadizing. Ben and some other boys. But he was the only one that got locked up. The others went home with their parents."

"Well that doesn't sound right. What were they vandalizing?"

"I don't know, Miss Connie. They wouldn't let me see my boy. Said I'd have to wait 'til the judge sets bail. The sheriff says he's going try to get bail set at $500. I don't have that kind of money, Miss Connie. I never have. My boy's just seventeen. He oughtn't be in jail. What am I going to do? What in the world am I going to do?" More sniffling, but Dilcey had herself under control.

"Get your hat and come with me is what. We're going to go down and see what fat old Nat McLeod thinks he's doing. You don't just go locking up young boys on a whim."

On the inside, Connie was not as brave as her words indicated. Nat McLeod called himself Chief of Police, even though the only other lawman in town was a deputy who helped direct traffic for large weddings, funerals, and the Fourth of July. McLeod was a fat slob. He was a stereotypical redneck, kept in office by the local political machine. But he knew the law. If he had Ben Reynolds in jail, he had a reason.

As she drove through the streets of Southport, she questioned Dilcey. Better to face Fat Nat with as much information as she could gather.

"He's a good boy, Miss Connie. So sweet, so thoughtful. It's all the fault of this instigation. I hate it. My boy was doing fine 'til he had to go to the instigated school."

"Do you mean 'integrated'?"

"Yes'm. That's what I said. Instigated. Anyway, when he went to the black school, all the teachers loved him. He was a leader, head of his class.

"Then the government started instigation and he had to go to the white school. Of a morning he rides the bus for an hour, just to get there. He could walk to his old school.

"He made good grades at the instigated school. He's a smart boy. But he's just one of a whole bunch of young'uns. His teachers don't notice him. He doesn't have any friends. He's so lonesome."

"I thought he was making some friends," Connie interjected.

"I thought so, too. But if he's making friends that land him in jail, he's not making the right friends."

Connie pulled her car to the curb in front of a mundane brick building. Located on Main Street, the jail was housed behind the police office. Dilcey jumped from the car and led Connie up the steps. When they entered, Nat McLeod's presence dominated the room.

"Dilcey. What you doing back here? I'm tired of your ugly face and your bawling. Git your black ass ... Oh howdy, Miz Edmonds." McLeod stood, making a futile attempt to fasten his shirt across his enormous belly. The office smelled of tobacco, body odor, and stale, greasy food.

"Don't 'howdy' me," Connie told McLeod. "And don't ever let me hear you talk to Mrs. Reynolds like that again. Not if you want to continue as a police officer in Southport. Now, why have you locked up her son?"

"Destruction of public property, Miz Edmonds. Destruction of public property. I arrested him last night. Caught him red-handed."

"And exactly what was he destroying?"

"Stop signs."

Connie's mouth fell open. "You put a seventeen-year-old, a juvenile, in jail for destroying stop signs? A boy who had never been in trouble before?"

Connie flinched when Nat McLeod reached to pat her on the shoulder. He used his most authoritative sheriff's voice to cover his thoughts. "Miz Edmonds. Why're you worrying your pretty head? This here's man's business. It don't concern you. You go on home and let the law take care of things."

Connie stared at him. She'd known what he was like. She'd voted for him anyway. Next election she wouldn't sit idly by and let him go unchallenged. But that was the future. Now she had to get Ben out of jail. She would have to talk to Nat McLeod with the only language he understood—power.

"McLeod. You have two sons who work for me. They will not have jobs tomorrow if you don't allow Mrs. Reynolds to see her own son. Immediately. And you will tell me why Ben was arrested and not the boys who were with him."

McLeod shrugged. He knew when he'd been beaten. He got his keys and led the way.

The young black boy sat alone in the last cell. Thank goodness for that. He hadn't spent the night with drunks and prostitutes. When he saw his mother his face lit up.

"Mommy," he cried, resorting to a term he hadn't used since he was six years old.

"It's okay, Bennie. Mommy's here." The small woman ran down the dimly lit hallway and grasped her son's hands through the bars. The two stood there, satisfied just to be together.

Connie blocked the chief's path as he tried to muscle his way toward the pair. Dilcey deserved time with her son. "Now, McLeod," she demanded. "Tell me the rest of the story. How come Ben was the only one arrested?"

"Because he was the perpetrator of the crime. The perpetrator." McLeod repeated the word to impress her. "The boys was driving through neighborhoods, throwing bottles at stop signs. Ben was the one throwing the bottles."

"And how do you know that?"

"Because the other boys said so. I received a report about 10 o'clock that a group of boys was joy-riding and smashing bottles. Sure 'nuff. I followed them with the lights off in the squad car. Soons I saw a bottle hit a sign, I pulled them over. And Ben was in the front seat."

"How many boys were in the car?"

"Six."

"So. Six boys, pitch dark. You arrest only Ben. Who were the other boys, Nat?"

"Jake Middlesbury, Tommy Spencer, Buddy—"

"That's what I thought. The mayor's son and a councilman's son. Lilly-livered offspring of your cronies. Those boys are all trouble. My guards chase them out of the lumberyard at least once a week."

"Their parents are all fine, upstanding—"

"Their parents keep you in this nice, cushy job. Now you release Ben in his mother's custody. You don't have the evidence to keep him."

"I can't do that, Miz Edmonds. I've got to hold him 'til the judge sets bail."

"Then you better figure out how you're going to support those six grandchildren of yours. Because their daddies sure won't be working for me tomorrow."

McLeod said no more. He walked the length of the hall and unlocked the cell. Then he turned and went in the bathroom. He wanted the whole stupid bunch out of his sight.

Connie drove the Reynolds to their home. Funny, in the five years she'd known Dilcey, she'd never seen where her maid lived.

The house was on the outskirts of Southport, in what was still called Brown Town. It was tiny. Connie couldn't imagine eight children growing up in such cramped quarters. Even in the dimming daylight, she could see that the outside needed painting. But it appeared neat and clean. Like Dilcey herself, the house exuded peace and warmth. Connie knew the children who lived there were well loved.

On the drive home, Ben spoke with bravado. "So I told that old sheriff, 'Fat Nat,' I says, 'you ain't got no cause to lock me up.'" But in her rearview mirror Connie noticed that Ben clung to his mother's hand for the entire drive.

Dilcey said nothing, content to hold her boy's hand and rejoice in his presence.

After the Reynolds had gone inside, Connie sat staring at the peeling paint and sagging shutters. Lucy had told her to get beyond herself, to help someone in need. Could this be a place to start? Dilcey must need assistance, trying to rear that many children.

And how about Ben? He was at a crossroads. What happened to him in the next few months would determine what sort of adult he would become.

Chapter 20

Visions and Signs

On Saturday morning Connie woke at sunrise, too excited to sleep. In two weeks they would be on Captain Bob's boat, heading for the party at Turtle Nest. Amazingly, she was looking forward to it. Her hospital stay and therapy with Marty must be working.

Jumping out of bed she put on her slippers and headed for the deck. Katie opened one eye, glaring at her as she left the bedroom. With definite cat disdain she snorted and snuggled deep into her pillow. "Humans," Connie could imagine her saying.

Her house faced west, so she never saw the sunrise. Rather, the marshes and brackish water began to glow rosy pink. As the sun ascended, this glow spread into the woodlands and onto trees. She preferred waking up this way. Her view was more a soft watercolor than a vibrant oil.

Already marsh life had begun the day's toil. A snowy egret stalked the mud, alternately lifting its spindly legs and spearing for fish. A flock of pelicans swooped low over her roofline, headed for the ocean and a day of fishing. Seeing so many birds must mean good fortune. "Happy fishing, guys," she shouted. Hordes of crickets provided steady, monotonous background music for her morning.

Connie settled onto a deck chair to watch the scenery and catnap. She had no idea how long she dozed, but was startled by a soft tap on the front door. Padding through the living room, she wondered who would be out so early. When she peered through the peephole she saw the strapping figure of Joe Johnston, St. Bettina's's caretaker and Nettie Mae's great-grandson. Opening the door, Connie welcomed him. "Come in, Mr. Johnston. Come in." Connie opened the door. "I know who you are. My mother speaks highly of you."

"Please call me Joe, Miss Edmonds. Everyone does—even my students, when they think I'm not listening."

Connie chuckled. "Teenagers. I think I was one, once. I'll call you Joe, but you must call me Connie. I'm having coffee on the deck. Will you join me?"

"Please. Just black."

When she brought Joe a steaming mug of hazelnut blend, Connie noted the peace on his face as he gazed across the marsh. "Ah, eastern North Carolina. There's no place like it. I teach biology in the high school, you know. I especially try to help my students learn to love the plants and wildlife of this region."

Connie wondered if she was in for a long discourse about biology. She remembered her mother saying that she had followed Joe around the gardens for hours before he would discuss Nettie Mae.

Instead, he got right to the point. "I would love to sit here all morning admiring your view, but I'm on my way to St. Bettina's. It gets too hot to do much in the garden after eleven o'clock. Anyway, my great-grandmother insisted I come."

"Nettie Mae?"

"Yes. I'm a little embarrassed to bother you. But you don't cross G.G.—great grandmother. If she sends you on an errand, you go."

"But she doesn't know me."

"No. But your mother mentioned you when she visited. G.G. says you've been on her mind ever since."

"How strange."

"It gets even stranger. You must understand that I have great respect for G.G. She's an intuitive, insightful woman. I've seen her cure people when the medical community has given up. I've had quite a bit of scientific education, so I'm a skeptic when something happens for no apparent reason. But I can't explain my G.G.'s powers. She can often predict the future—when it's going to rain, that sort of thing. And she dreams dreams. Lately, she's been dreaming about you."

"Me?"

"Yes. You and Suzanne Marshburn. The girl your mother was asking about."

Connie rose and walked across the deck to stare at the water. Should she throw him out? His G.G. was a quack, no doubt about that. But Joe Johnston was an educated man. He would not have come if he weren't sincere. And this whole business with Suzanne had already been fraught with mystery and coincidence.

Setting her coffee mug on the weathered planks of the railing, she appreciated their roughness. The boards were a mainstay of stability in what had suddenly become surreal.

"Please continue, Mr. Johnston—Joe," she said, turning to face him.

"Of course, dreams are vague. Often one thing in a dream symbolizes something else. So my G.G. leaves that to your interpretation. But Suzanne has been appearing once or twice a week. At first she didn't speak. Dream figures are like that. It's as if they have to decide if they can trust their host.

"Then she identified herself. Just said her name was Suzanne. But she was dressed in clothes of the 1800s. She kept saying, 'Forgive yourself. Don't waste your life with blame for another's death. I did, and I was foolish.'

"When G.G. asked who the message was for, Suzanne said, 'Helen's daughter. The one with auburn hair.' Then she vanished and hasn't returned. G.G. thought of all the Helens she knew. None of their daughters have auburn hair. Black people generally don't, you know. When your mother came and said her name was Helen, G.G. remembered the dream. That's why she asked what color hair you had."

"Tell me again what Suzanne said." Connie's mouth was so dry she could barely speak.

"Forgive yourself. Don't waste your life with blame for another's death. I did, and I was foolish. Does that mean anything to you, Connie?"

"Yes. Yes it does. I'm just not sure what. We do know Suzanne blamed herself for John Marshburn's death. The note in Mother's mahogany chest proves that."

"And one more thing," Joe added as an afterthought. "G.G. says you are to come to her if you need to. That's quite an honor as she's never invited a white person to her home before."

Joe excused himself then, saying he had azaleas to mulch. Connie, though shaken by his message, knew his intentions were good. She thanked him as she opened the front door. As he was leaving, she remembered Ben Reynolds. Joe must know him since he taught at the high school.

"Sure. I know Ben. Kind of quiet. Seems like a nice kid. Why do you ask?"

Connie briefed Joe on Ben's recent brush with the law. "His mother works for me, Joe. She worries about him a great deal. Is there any way I could help Ben?"

"Let me think about it, Connie. I'll ask some of the teachers at school. Maybe they'll have some ideas. I'll get back to you."

After Joe left, Connie returned to the deck. Could it be true? Could Suzanne really be sending her a message from the grave? She had always scoffed at voodoo and black magic. But the coincidences were ominous.

What else had Suzanne said? "Don't waste your life like I did," or something to that effect. Connie had never considered the similarities, but there they were. Both she and Suzanne had been directly or indirectly responsible for another's death. And Captain Cogdill's diary suggested his daughter might have loved a priest. Marty and Lucy said that she herself was wasting her life with blame. Evidentially, Suzanne had done that too. Was it as Lucy believed? Was she was afraid of Robin's collar? Figuring that out would take a great deal more thought.

Chapter 21

Souls Reborn

Joe kept his word. He talked to his fellow teachers about Ben Reynolds. The school guidance counselor suggested a job. "Often that helps a young man," she advised. "Gives them pocket change and keeps them occupied."

On Monday morning Robin, Connie, and Joe discussed the situation over coffee. "Well, I suppose you need help in the gardens," Robin said to Joe. "But the church can't afford it. We're stretched to the limit with the restoration project."

Animated, Connie clapped her hands. "I think it's a wonderful idea, Robin. Let me donate the salary. Lucy says helping others redeems the soul or something to that effect. It won't cost all that much. Please, let me do it. Just don't tell Ben."

So Father Robin Benson contracted with Ben Reynolds for ten hours of work per week in the gardens of St. Bettina's Church.

At first Ben had resisted. "I ain't gonna do like you and work at no honky church," he shouted at Joe. "Even if it is just your summer job." But when Robin convinced Nat McLeod to drop vandalism charges in exchange for community service, Ben capitulated.

On Tuesday, Ben reported for work—ill tempered and sullen. Joe paid him no mind. After years of teaching moody teenagers, he recognized a bluff when he saw one. Something was eating at Ben. Something bigger than "working at the honky church," as he phrased it. Joe bided his time, he'd find out soon enough. Kids talked to him, eventually.

"Hold the gardening spade at an angle Ben." Joe took the shovel and demonstrated. "It goes in the ground much easier." The teenager scowled, but redirected his tool.

"So, what courses are you taking in school next year?" Joe asked.

"Nothinmuch," Ben mumbled in reply.

"I'm sorry. I didn't catch that?"

"Nothing much. I said I ain't taking nothing much."

"But it's your senior year. Aren't you excited about graduation? Aren't you taking courses for college?"

"Naw. Naw I ain't." Ben scowled again and stalked off to chop weeds.

Joe had come upon his first clue. Something about graduation—a scary time for kids. Suddenly cut loose from familiar surroundings, they were expected to survive. Coming from a fatherless family of eight, Ben fell heir to few options. That, combined with his lonely night in jail, must weigh heavy on his thoughts.

Joe said no more until lunch. Ben weeded the entire walk leading to the church sanctuary. Impressed, Joe complimented his helper.

"Ben, you did a fine job on that walkway. It would have taken me all day.... Good Lord! Hold still! There's a snake wrapped around your neck!"

In spite of himself, Ben chuckled. "Aw, go on, Mr. Johnston. You ain't afraid of a little green snake, are you? And you a biology teacher. This here's Petey, he's my pet. I've had him more'n a year now."

"Your pet?"

"Yessir. I brought him in this old shoebox. That's where he lives. I let him out to keep me company while I was weeding."

"Keep you company?" Joe realized he was not functioning as the adult in this situation. But the idea of a snake twined around the boy's shoulders dumbfounded him.

"Yessir. He's good company. Don't never complain or go yakking all the time like humans. He just sits on my shoulders. Sometimes he takes a nap, sometimes he catches bugs. Mostly, he just sits there."

They finished their lunch in silence. Joe remained nervous throughout the meal. Digesting his sandwich with snake eyes glaring at him proved difficult. Petey scrutinized the biology teacher—periodically flicking his long, forked tongue.

Ben was enjoying his teacher's discomfort. The stony shell of bitterness thinned. Maybe this guy was okay after all. The kids at school liked him.

"I got lots of animals at home, Mr. Johnston," he ventured. I got a bird that flies down from the trees and eats out of my hand. I whistle to her when I get home and she flies right down. I got a three-legged hamster and a guinea pig. And me and my brothers and sisters got four dogs and two cats."

"Why do you keep so many animals, Ben?"

"Well, I done thought on that. I guess it's 'cause animals don't ask much. They just need a little food and water. Mostly they want attention. I ain't got no friends. The animals keep me company."

Ben mumbled the last into the collar of his blue plaid shirt. But Joe knew he was gaining the boy's confidence.

The afternoon passed pleasantly after Ben put Petey in the shoebox. Man and boy fell into the easy communication of two souls who love the land and its creatures.

"I had you going there, didn't I, Mr. Johnston?" Ben teased. "Wait 'til I get back to school and tell the kids the biology teacher is scared of snakes."

"If you do, don't take biology next year. You won't get out of my class with a passing grade."

Fascinated with the excavation at the slave gravesite, Ben spent his break time leaning against his shovel, questioning the young archaeologists. *Connie's right,* Joe thought watching the boy. *Ben deserved their help. He's too bright to be in trouble with the likes of Nat McLeod.*

At four o' clock, Joe released Ben from his chores. Satisfied with the day's work, he again complimented the boy. "Thanks, Ben. You're a good worker. See you tomorrow."

Ben smiled shyly and reached under a huge azalea for his hoe. "Dear Lordy!" he cried, retracting his hand and falling onto his knees in the grass.

Joe heard his gasp as he walked toward the church. Fearing he had encountered another snake, one much more fierce than Petey, he hurried toward him. "What is it, Ben?" he shouted.

"Sh-h-h. Be still. Look."

Ben parted the thicket of azalea branches. A small gray rabbit huddled in a clump of grass beneath the flowering bush. One mangled ear hung against its cheek and bloody skin glistened through wounds obviously made by the claws of a larger animal. The rabbit trembled with fear, staring at them with dull, pain-crazed eyes.

"Good Lord," whispered Joe. "It's been attacked by something. Probably a wild dog. We better kill it and put it out of its misery." Joe raised his shovel.

"The hell you say!" Ben dropped the branches and pushed the older man aside. He shot Joe a look of hatred that said the confidence built that afternoon was gone. "You ain't gonna kill it. You'll have to kill me first."

"But Ben, it's suffering. It's in pain. Killing it would be merciful."

"You ain't gonna kill it! You hear me?" Ben shouted at Joe with the quavering anger of a little boy trying to sound like a man.

"All right, Ben. Calm down. I won't kill it. But the animal needs help."

Ben didn't answer. Instead he took off his shirt and knelt on the grass. With infinite gentleness he reached beneath the bush and wrapped the animal in the soft cloth. Then he sat on the grass, stroking it and speaking in a strange, soothing language.

They stayed that way for at least five minutes. Gradually the terrified rabbit stopped trembling. Its eyes closed and it nestled against Ben's arm.

"Let me take it home, Mr. Johnston. I can make it better, I know I can. I have a way with animals. I'm always patching them up one way or another."

"Well you've certainly calmed that little fellow. Sure, go ahead and try. He's got nothing to lose."

Ben made a strange sight leaving the garden. Bare chested, he carried a wounded rabbit in one arm and a box with a snake inside in the other. Joe pondered the irony as they left the cobblestone walk and skirted the statue of a benevolent St. Francis of Assisi with the wild animals that he loved.

Ben named his rabbit Luke. "Maybe the name'll help you get better. Mama says St. Luke was a doctor in the Bible." The next day, Luke replaced Petey in the shoebox. Joe rejoiced since he preferred the company of a sick rabbit to that of a snake.

When questioned, Ben became philosophical. "Well, at first Petey didn't like the idea. But I told him I couldn't tend to him and Luke, and get my work done. So he says it's okay if he stays home for awhile."

The next few days passed in relative tranquility. Ben worked hard, checking on Luke at regular intervals. He would lift the animal from the box and entice it with grass or a bit of carrot. Although its wounds were healing, the ear still listed awkwardly to one side. A lopsided ear would probably mark Luke for life.

But Ben was worried. "He ain't getting well, Mr. Johnston. He drinks a little water, but he ain't eating. I ain't never had this trouble with my animals before."

"Where's this rabbit that's been rescued from the fierce claws of death?" Connie and Wayne Bailey crossed the mossy churchyard. They'd tried to stay in touch since she'd left the hospital, but their work schedules made that difficult. This afternoon had been planned for two weeks.

Connie and Joe had discussed Ben's progress daily. Today she told Wayne she'd like to stop by the church and check on him.

"Here's someone who may help you, Ben," said Connie. "This is Mr. Wayne Bailey. He's a nurse over at the hospital. But he's leaving next month for medical school."

Wayne stooped and stroked the animal's soft fur. "You've done a fine job with his wounds, Ben. He's healing nicely."

"He won't eat, Mr. Bailey. I can't get him to eat."

Wayne lifted the little animal. It sat alone and forlorn in the great hand, the dull, faraway look still haunting its eyes. Wayne could feel bony ribs barely covered by fur. "Connie says that you think he was attacked by a wild dog?"

"That's what we think," Joe answered. "I've seen packs of them roaming the woods behind the church. I'd say one got hold of this little fellow."

Wayne gently set the rabbit back on the ground. "My guess is he's still traumatized from that. Sometimes you can heal the body but not the spirit."

"What can I do, Mr. Bailey?" Ben's voice pleaded. "Luke can't die. He just can't."

"You're doing all you can, Ben. Keep trying to feed him and talk to him. And pray. Sometimes it just takes a miracle."

But Luke got no better. Ben did his work, peeking frequently into the cardboard box. Joe saw sadness creep into the boy's eyes each time he shut the lid.

Ben had just looked into the shoebox for the fifteenth time that morning. This time anger, rather than sadness, coursed through the taunt young body. He threw his shovel to the ground, grabbed the shoebox, and hurried toward the church. "Dang it. I got to try," he shouted to no one in particular.

"Ben, stop. Where're you going? You can't interrupt Father Robin." Joe caught up with the boy. Grabbing his shoulder he reprimanded, "Father Robin and Connie are working. He doesn't like to be interrupted if he's concentrating."

"Well I don't care. I got to talk to him. I got to talk to him 'bout Luke."

"Stop it Ben. Father Robin will—"

"What in the name of St. Cecilia is going on out here? You two sound like a barroom brawl." Robin looked down at them from the top of the church steps; Connie peered over his shoulder. "Father Robin," Ben cried. "You got to help Luke. You just got to. He ain't getting no better. I've done all I can. You got to help him."

Robin descended the few steps to the stone walkway. Resting his hand on the boy, he signaled for the Joe to release his grip.

"Ben, Ben. Calm down. What's this about me helping Luke? I understand you've done a fine job tending to him."

"But he ain't getting no better, Father. He ain't eating. There's nothing else I can do. But you can. Mr. Bailey said for us to pray. That's your job."

"You want me to pray for Luke?"

"I see on the church sign you have healing services. That's what Luke needs. You got to do a healing service for him. And you got to do it right now!"

"Ben!" Joe admonished. "Father Robin can't do a healing service for a rabbit. Don't be ridiculous."

"Yes he can." Ben stomped his foot in determination. "My Mama says Jesus loves all critters. So if Father Robin prays for Him to heal people, why can't he pray for Luke?"

Robin studied the boy. What he said made perfect sense. But he had never had much success with his healing services. Every Wednesday he prayed for the same people, for the same aches and pains. Afterward, everyone left for lunch at the Southport Diner, saying they felt better. But he'd seen no miraculous cures.

"Please, Father Robin." Ben interrupted his thoughts. "My Mama prays for us children when we gets sick. Please pray for Luke."

"All right, Ben. With faith like yours, how can I say no? Let me go inside for my prayer book and the holy oil."

"I'm leaving, Robin," Connie said. She wanted no part in a healing service, even one for a rabbit.

"Oh no, Miss Edmonds. You can't go." Ben grabbed her arm and drew her back into the group. "The Good Book says when two or three is gathered together, Jesus will grant their heart's desire. You got to pray with us."

"He has a point, Connie. I'll be right back." Robin left them on the walk. Soon he returned carrying his worn prayer book, a vial of holy oil, and a white cloth.

Ben lifted the lid of Luke's shoebox. When Robin reached for the small animal, it gave no sign of life. A faint thump against his fingers proved its heart still beat, otherwise, it sat immobile.

Robin, Ben, Connie, and Joe formed a circle on the church lawn. Rustling magnolia leaves provided the only sound until Robin's deep voice began the ancient liturgy.

Connie listened as Robin read The Communion of the Sick from the 1928 *Book of Common Prayer*. She thought how appropriate the words were for this tiny creature so near death, and was vaguely comforted. "O Lord, Holy Father, by whose loving-kindness our souls and bodies are renewed; mercifully look upon this thy servant, that, every cause of sickness being removed, he may be restored to soundness of health, through Jesus Christ our Lord. Amen."

When he finished, Robin dipped his finger in holy oil and traced the sign of the cross on the miniscule forehead. "That's all I can do, Ben. The rest is up to God." Robin gently set Luke back in his box.

Connie sighed. *What a shame to get Ben's hopes up. Probably this extra exertion and handling would be the end of the little creature.* The rabbit sat still, a faraway look in its glazed eyes. Suddenly, shaking its head as if waking from a nightmare, Luke burrowed in the grass pile. Feebly it grasped a bit of clover in its forepaws and began nibbling. Connie's stumbled against Wayne in amazement. *Could it be? Could some sort of divine intervention have actually taken place?*

"I think it's enough, Father Robin," shouted Ben. "I think Jesus done healed Luke. Hallelujah. Thank you, Jesus!"

Robin regarded the animal in amazement. "I don't understand. I've prayed and prayed for members of my congregation, with no results. Yet when I pray for this little rabbit, he gets better."

Ben shook his head in disgust. "Father Robin, you may be a preacher man, but you sure don't know much. My mama says we ain't supposed to decide how God works. We just pray and leave the rest up to Him."

Tired of so much theology, Ben handed the rabbit box to Joe. After three joyous strides, he cart-wheeled across the churchyard. His shouts of "Hallelujah" echoed through the old magnolias and across the tombstones of the sleeping dead.

Connie was the only one not rejoicing. She distanced herself from the group. The strangest sensation had come over her as Robin had prayed for Luke. It concerned Ben. Somehow she knew the boy must become a veterinarian. That seemed an impossible dream, but perhaps not. Again, she would consult Joe Johnston. But if Ben were to attend vet school, his attitude and grammar would need concentrated attention.

Chapter 22

▼

Love and Betrayal

When Connie arrived home, Blake Benson, her postman, was standing on her porch, scrutinizing a large parcel.

As Connie approached he looked up, curiosity blanketing his face. "Big package here for you, Connie. From England." Blake handed her a manila envelope, then waited impatiently to view its contents.

Connie retrieved the package and studied the postmark. "It's from my mother," she told Blake. "She's in Europe, you know."

"Well, open it," Blake cajoled. "Let's see what she sent."

"Not now, Blake. I need to go inside." Connie smiled and turned toward the house, leaving a clearly disappointed Blake alone on her steps.

Once inside, Connie set her purse on the table, closed a squeaky shutter, and began pacing the room in anticipation of what she was about to read. These must be the letters Suzanne Marshburn had written to her father over a century ago. She had waited eagerly ever since her mother had promised to send them.

Despite her agitation, she resisted the urge to sit in the middle of the floor and begin reading. She had chores to do before she could afford that luxury. Katie needed feeding, the message button on the telephone blinked, and she should fix her supper.

An hour later, she carried the parcel and a cup of tea to her deck. Hues from the dying sun filtered muted light across her table and deck chairs. She would read here until dark, then move inside.

A bundle of letters, ten in all, fell from the manila envelope onto the rough wooden surface of her picnic table. Connie was surprised there were so few, considering they covered a period of over a year. Then she remembered that a war was being fought. Whatever Suzanne shipped to her father had to be smuggled out on blockade runners from Wilmington.

Connie had visited the museum in Wilmington and seen diagrams of the Union naval blockade, which extended from Washington, D.C. around the coast of Florida to New Orleans. The blockade was established to strangle the Confederacy. The South exported cotton to European ports, trading it for necessities. By blockading coastal ports with powerful naval vessels, the Union planned to sever the lifeline linking the South to their suppliers.

Eventually the plan worked. But from the beginning of the blockade in April 1861, until the fall of the Confederacy in early 1865, sleek blockade runners eluded larger, slower, Union vessels. These boats were fast, small, and drew little water. They could dart between Yankee ships, race for shore, then hide in creeks and canals. The work was dangerous and became more so as the Union tightened its stranglehold. Many brave Southern sailors and much cargo were lost when a blockade runner capsized, ran aground, or was bombarded by Yankee guns. Suzanne's letters had traveled fearful miles before reaching Captain Cogdill.

The envelopes were brown with age, encircled by a faded blue ribbon. When Connie released the knot, the letters spilled before her like dried old women with stories to tell.

Mice had made lunch on the corners of several. As she removed the first page, its edges crumbled to dust on the table. Connie realized she was handling historical material. Perhaps when she finished she would donate the letters to the museum in Wilmington.

Suzanne's handwriting was precise and flowery. Often a word was not decipherable because of curly cues and decorations. The ink had faded to sepia brown. Language was archaic, spellings quite different from modern English, paragraphs and punctuation almost nonexistent.

Arranging the letters in chronological order, she decided to read start to finish. The first was dated July 10, 1863, the last, November 15, 1864. As Connie began each letter, she carefully removed it from its envelope, shook off one hundred years of dust, and spread it before her. When she finished, she did not stuff the paper back into its casing, preferring to file letter and envelope together. A museum expert would best know how to handle the deteriorating parchment.

Sunset afforded an hour of light. When darkness made her task impossible, Connie gathered the papers and moved to her kitchen table.

At some point it became necessary to take notes. Facts and figures, names and dates, began to clamor through her brain like children demanding attention.

Details of household life filled the pages. Because John Marshburn had died in 1859, Suzanne was left a young widow, trying to support herself and three children as war threatened her home. Connie read of Suzanne releasing the slaves, more an economic necessity than a benevolent one. Some of the freedmen ran away or joined the Union or Confederate armies. Only Lila, the children's nursemaid, and her fun-loving husband Joel, stayed with the family. Suzanne wrote that she couldn't have survived without them:

> ... *Lila or I tend the children, offering Joel what little assistance we are able. We have made preparations for winter. Joel planted a small garden. He is all* [illegible] *and resourceful but alas cannot resolve our grave dilemma.*
> *My beloved friend Rose Greenhow—you will recall making her acquaintance when you visited at Marshlands—procured a bolt of linsey-woolsey for us. Joel, Lila the children and myself shall all dress alike this winter. We have ripped the carpet to* [illegible] *shoes.*
> *Our lives are at the whim and mercy of whichever army occupies the land. They take charge of Marshlands affording us little decency and privacy. Our chickens and livestock have been slaughtered and they* [illegible] *the furniture.*
> *Would I could inform you our deplorable state of affairs was improved. I know dear Father it grieves you to read these words. We will survive with God's grace and the aid of Lila and Joel. Pray for us my Father. And pray this dreadful conflict will cease and we* [illegible] *to some form of normalcy.*
>
> *Your loving Daughter*
> *Suzanne Cogdill Marshburn*
> *Sept. 21, 1863*

In another letter, Suzanne wrote at length about her friend, Rose O'Neal Greenhow.

> *My Dear Father,*
>
> *I was cheered by the news that you and Rose spent a pleasant evening dining and [illegible] the theatre. You wrote she just returned from France and had the honor of an audience with the Emperor. Perhaps she [illegible] her little daughter? She resides in a convent school in Paris.*
>
> *Rose denies me intimate knowledge of her pursuits and activities though I harbor my speculations. She [illegible] my protection and safety. I fear she is aiding the South. I know she and her daughter were imprisoned in their home in Washington and later in the Old Capital Prison. Now you [illegible] she was received at Court by the Queen and dined with Mr. Carlysle—a known Advocate of the Confederacy. Is she promoting sympathy and soliciting currency? I fathom from her travels she journeys through the blockade. That is how she disposes of my few and pitiful possessions and procures supplies for our comfort and sustenance.*
>
> *Please write what you know Dear Father. I fear for her safety. She is my loyal and trusted friend. As you ken I have no sympathies—Union or Confederate. I would perform any act a gracious God deigned in my power to hasten the ending of this dastardly conflict. My desire is to be left in Peace to my life and that of my children. And to know the dawning of the day when Mothers and Wives, Sisters and Little Children shall be reunited with their men folk in the bosom of loving Families.*
>
> *Ever your loving Daughter*
Suzanne
Marshlands
March 16, 1864

Connie read all night. Around dawn, she rested her head on her forearm and slept until the glare of morning sun woke her. Stretching, she searched for Katie. The spotted cat slept in her chair. As soon as she realized her mistress was awake, she began demanding breakfast. As she fed the irascible cat, Connie remembered the letters. She had read them all. Each was more pitiful, more desperate than the last.

Union ships strangled the South with the blockade. In August 1864, the port of Mobile, Alabama fell to Admiral Farragut. In September, General William Tecumseh Sherman captured Atlanta and began his scorch and burn march to the sea. Suzanne, like many other Southerners, grew more hopeless with each passing day.

Then Connie remembered the final letter. Involuntarily, she shuddered. That letter was the most troubling. Not troubling—horrific. She could not reread it, not without Robin's wisdom and discernment.

Connie knew he would be in his office, polishing his sermon and answering correspondence. Placing the last letter in a file folder, she shooed Katie onto the porch and walked the few blocks to the church.

It was a lovely, temperate day. The wind blowing off the water made the air almost balmy, caressing cheeks, teasing nostrils, promising a day of sunlight, salt air, and sea breeze. Designed by its Creator to lift any mood, Connie hardly noticed. Her mind was occupied, her spirit troubled.

As she walked, she compared her peace, her well being, to that of Suzanne Marshburn's at the end of the Civil War. She strolled the streets of Southport in freedom, her every need assured before she asked. In contrast, Suzanne had been mentally and spiritually exhausted, worried about her children, probably hungry. Four years of war and privation had broken her will.

Robin was pleasantly surprised when Connie tapped on the door. "Come in. Come in," he said, opening the door for her. "I'm polishing a little homily about Ben's faith and Luke's healing. I'll use it in a sermon someday."

The priest fell silent when he saw Connie's face. Her slumped shoulders and slow gait showed she carried a heavy burden. Taking her arm, he steered her to a chair. "What is it, Connie?"

As she handed him the folder, she sighed. "Don't read it, I'll summarize. It takes hours to decipher. I spent last night wading through this letter and others like it."

That explained the red eyes and dark circles. But there was more—a heaviness, a sadness foreign to Connie's usual persona.

Robin opened the folder and saw a letter dated November 1, 1864. He knew Connie had been waiting for her mother to send Suzanne Marshburn's letters from England. Settling back in his office chair, he waited for her to begin.

Taking a deep breath, she started. What difference did it make now, anyway, so long ago. It was just sad, so sad.

"They endured such hardships, Robin—hunger, theft, even fear for their lives. Suzanne's friend, Rose O'Neal Greenhow, was her only ally. She smuggled the Marshburn silver through the blockade, then returned with much needed supplies for the family."

"I remember Rose Greenhow," said Robin. "Hattie O'Brien mentioned her. She was a spy, wasn't she?"

"Yes, she was a beautiful woman who charmed Northern statesmen and generals, then carried their secrets to Confederate troops.

But toward the end of the war Suzanne became so tired, so alone, desperate and scared. That's what I read about in the last letter."

Leaning forward, Connie spoke in a whisper. She knew she had read a letter never intended for eyes other than those of an adoring parent. One who could absolve a child any sin.

"By September of 1864, Suzanne realized Rose was a spy and a staunch Southern supporter. She reminded her father that he had written of audiences with influential politicians—opportunities Rose had used to argue for English intervention on behalf of the Confederacy. He had told Suzanne of the publication of Rose's memoirs which were widely read in Europe and had raised much currency for the Southern cause. 'Her efforts, dear father,' Connie quoted, 'serve to prolong what I fear has become a hopeless conflict.'

"As you see, the last letter was written in November, 1864, after Rose's death and funeral. It describes the funeral, but it also tells about Suzanne's part in her friend's drowning."

Connie began to cry. Her life had become entwined with that of Suzanne Marshburn's. Empathy, imagination, pain transported her to a cold beach on a day 114 years earlier.

Robin came and stood beside her, but he sensed Connie was no longer with him in the room. When she spoke again her voice was strained and cracked. She used Suzanne's words, from a scene played out long ago.

"Joel came running to the house. 'Miz Suzanne, Miz Suzanne,' he hollered. 'Dere's a runner gone aground in de river. It be stuck on a sandbar. I could take you dere, Miz Suzanne. I could git you dere in no time.'

"My heart sank. Rose might be on that runner. Certainly there were other poor souls who would die in the mouth of our own Cape Fear River.

"Joel harnessed the team and helped me up. At breakneck speed we raced for the river. It was almost twilight. A runner was indeed stranded on a sandbar. Behind it, tall masts of Union warships closed in like gallows straining for their victim.

"I saw the name on the runner. *The Condor*. A name I will remember until the day I die. You must understand, it was nearly dark. The mist and fog lessened our visibility even more. Suddenly a lifeboat was lowered. We saw, I think we saw, a woman raise her skirts and climb aboard. Joel whispered, 'Lordy, Miz Suzanne. Could dat be Miz Rose?'

"I didn't know. Father had told me she would soon return. Her book had sold well and she was bringing much needed gold currency to the Confederacy. I knew if that were Rose, she would have the gold on her person.

"At first, the lifeboat made progress. We thought it would reach shore. But the waves were too rough. The sea was wild, spewing foam like demons from Hell clutching for the occupants of the laboring vessel.

"Joel shouted at me. 'Let me go, Miz Suzanne. I be a strong swimmer. If dat's Miz Rose I can bring her to shore. Or whoever it be. Let me go, Miz Suzanne.' Joel was hopping up and down on the beach, waiting for me to approve the rescue. He was a free man but he'd been a slave all his life. Poor thing, he wouldn't act without an order.

"I couldn't bring myself to let him go. I put my hand on his arm and whispered, 'No.' Once I prayed that God would let me aid the end of this war. What sort of cruel and vengeful deity would demand the death of my dearest friend to fulfill that prayer?

"Within five minutes the lifeboat flipped over. We saw the woman once, when a whitecap crested the beach. Her long black skirts pulled her down as the wave sucked her back to its bosom. Joel was crying, 'Oh, Lordy. It be Miz Rose. I knows it be Miz Rose. Oh, Lordy forgive us.'

"By then the last rays of sunlight were gone. We could see no more. The sea boomed a loud, hollow crescendo, as if pounding out a funeral dirge. Joel and I climbed into the carriage and drove home. He cried all the way.

"That was Rose on the lifeboat. Her body washed ashore the next morning. The gold from her book was sewn into her skirt and in a reticule secured around her neck. That's what had dragged her down to Poseidon's graveyard.

"Jake Bell from town rode out to tell me. He knew Rose and I were friends. He need not have come. I already knew.

"I went to her funeral. She looked beautiful, so peaceful, just as if she were asleep. Wax candles surrounded the corpse; flowers in crosses and bouquets overflowed the casket. Hundreds of townspeople and reverent soldiers filed by to pay respects to their heroine. A huge Confederate flag draped the bier. Above all, an ebony crucifix stood sentinel.

"She lay in state until two o'clock. Then the body was moved to the Catholic Church of St. Thomas. The Reverend Dr. Corcoran delivered her funeral oration. He praised her heroism and patriotic devotion, but warned us of the uncertainty of all ambitions, even though they be admirable.

"The coffin, still draped with the Confederate flag, was borne to Oakdale Cemetery. A large funeral cortege followed, in spite of the rain that drenched us. As her coffin was lowered into its grave, the sun broke forth in all its glory and a rainbow spanned the horizon.

"I pray this is an omen for my dear Rose. I pray she finds peace in God's kingdom. Forgive me for not aiding you in this lifetime, my sister. It was not to you I refused aid, but to this dreaded war. Forgive me, my sister."

Connie slumped against Robin, her story ended. Perspiration soaked her brow as her limp body conformed to his strong one. Spent, she rested in the security of his arms.

Chapter 23

Complications

Robin brought Connie tea. He watched as she sipped, strength slowly seeping back into her body. Light from the afternoon sun played across her auburn hair. The tension slipped from her face, leaving a certain vulnerability in its place. Once again he realized how much he loved her.

He made up his mind. He would do it. But not now. This decision would affect the rest of their lives. They were both too exhausted for that, maybe tonight. Yes, that would work.

"Connie, could I drop by tonight with final plans for the renovation of the interior of the church?" he asked.

"Sure. Come over. But you know the Turtle Nest party is in two days. Janie Kilpatrick has stored all the rubber turtles in my living room. If you can stand that, you're welcome."

Robin arrived at seven o'clock with sheaves of paper under his arm. He spread these on her living room floor. Lowering his lanky frame to her carpet, he stretched his long legs out beside the papers. Taking her hand, he pulled her to him and positioned her in front of the first drawing.

"As you can see, we're making few changes in the interior of the church. We want it to look and feel as it has for the past one hundred years. Only a keen observer will know we've moved a few pews—opened the area and increased seating capacity."

"What about the flags?" asked Connie. You are keeping the flags."

"Certainly. We'd have armed revolt if we didn't. And they're vital to our church's history. Here. They're shown in this drawing." Robin retrieved a second sheet. "They'll be cleaned and mended. Should any disintegrate during cleaning, they'll be replaced."

"What's this?" Connie noticed a small sketch of sailing ships, sea life, an unusual looking cross.

"That's the needlepoint pattern the ladies are using for prayer cushions. The cross is the seafarer's cross, an old design revered by sailors. The ships, crabs, fish, and shrimp represent Southport's dependence on the ocean. God has blessed us with manna from the sea just as Moses' followers were blessed with manna from Heaven. Our women are celebrating that with their exquisite needlework."

Again Connie marveled at the change in this quiet man as he spoke of his church. She'd seen that change earlier, when Robin had prayed for Luke. The man had transcended himself, become more than a small town priest praying in a garden. It was as if a fire, a presence, had control and was using him to convey a message. His voice had taken on a luster not present in ordinary speech. Connie had no words to describe the look on his face—a mixture of peace and power. Something very old and vibrant.

Katie, however, was not interested in plans for the church or in analyzing its priest. She stood at the back door and scratched until her mistress rose and let her out. When Connie returned, she sat on the floor and nestled against Robin.

Robin was lost in thought, staring at the floor. They sat this way for a good five minutes, wrapped in the warmth of each other. Again Connie felt the comfort, the safety and security of being with this man. Maybe this was what Lucy meant when she said Charlie was the anchor in her life.

Finally, Robin took her hand and met her eyes. "Connie, I've told you before. These past few months have been the happiest I've ever known. Basically, I'm a loner. But you've brought such joy to my life, opened windows I didn't know existed. I want to know this joy as long as I live. I was wondering if, well ... I was wondering if you'd marry me."

Connie gulped. This was too much, coming on the heels of Lucy's questions when she'd visited in New Bern. She hadn't answered those yet. She knew she loved Robin, but was she ready for a lifetime commitment? No. Not yet. Too many ghosts still haunted the shadows of her mind.

"I, well ... ah," she finally stammered.

"Surely this isn't a complete surprise." Robin's tone was persuasive, pleading, a quality she'd never heard before. "We've spent lots of time together. We have fun. And you did say you loved me."

"I do love you, Robin. That's not the question." Connie stoked his cheek for emphasis. "The problem is me. I'm afraid. Of what, I'm not quite sure. Commitment, certainly. But something else as well. I think it's all tied up with this Suzanne Marshburn thing and me forgiving myself over Amanda Roberts' death. Lucy says I'm afraid to marry a priest because that would be like marrying God."

Connie realized she was botching what had seemed logical at the time. Since she hadn't processed her own thoughts, hadn't discussed them with Marty Connors, she was doing a poor job of conveying them to Robin.

As she spoke, Robin's face changed from hope to barely suppressed rage. His eyes darkened, deep furrows interlaced his brow. The little muscles around his mouth tightened, twitching as he spat out his next words.

"What you're saying is you're too good to be a clergyman's wife, is that it? Fear, my foot. You're afraid all right, afraid you'll have to change your fancy lifestyle. I know I'm not as exciting as those successful men from Raleigh and Charlotte you've dated. I was foolish enough to hope you preferred something more sedate. How stupid of me."

Robin hastily gathered his sketches, knocking over a lamp in the process. He strode to the door and banged through the screen. It slammed with a resounding whack. "Call me if you have a change of heart," he shouted over his shoulder. "Otherwise, I won't bother you again."

Connie stared down the walk long after Robin left. How could he be so cruel? She remembered his reaction to Jack Tully's television interview at the slave graves and his subsequent confession; he'd displayed an almost uncontrollable temper. Sure, she'd done a poor job of explaining why she wasn't ready for marriage. That was no excuse. This man was a priest. He should be able to understand. Maybe he wasn't as perfect as she'd thought.

Chapter 24

Turtle Nest

July 4, 1977 dawned hot and muggy. Connie was up at sunrise, anxious to get an early start for Turtle Nest. It would be rewarding to see the result of the hard work done by Janie and her staff. Also she could socialize with friends from across the state. Then she remembered Robin. How would he act after having asked her to marry him? Would they speak? She had no clue.

Connie was still furious that he had so misunderstood her reasons for not being ready for marriage. He had jumped to conclusions about what she wanted in a man. Sure, she didn't explain things as well as Lucy. But he had no right to overreact as he had.

It never occurred to Connie that it had taken all of Robin's courage to ask the question. When the answer was not an immediate "yes," he had felt threatened. He had crawled back into a protective shell, then wrapped the cloak of anger around himself for protection.

Connie had made a special trip to the shops in Raleigh for her outfit. Of course, it had to be red, white, and blue. And cool. She must look calm and cool all day. She had finally chosen crisp, white Ann Taylor Bermuda shorts with a matching red and blue knit top. There was a wide band of blue around the neckline. Here she attached the Turtle Nest pin and logo.

Slipping her feet into her blue thongs, she turned to her full length mirror. Not bad for an almost fifty-year-old woman. The white shorts accented her bronze skin. Hours of reading or working on her deck had tanned her arms and legs to a golden brown. Never one to spend time basking in the sun, she found she tanned easily as she went about her daily routine. She knew she was lucky, most auburn-haired people burned or freckled in the summertime.

She caught her hair in a clump, twisted it, then fastened it on top of her head with a large clip. There, that would keep it off her neck and be cool. Reaching for her perfume, she changed her mind. No, the sweet smell would attract bugs and mosquitoes. Instead she doused herself with odorless bug spray. She had authorized Janie to order seventy cans of spray for the party. Her guests would appreciate that. The island was home to many pests as well as beautiful wildlife.

Connie met her staff at the Southport boat dock at nine o'clock. As soon as the group assembled, she made a short speech. "Everyone knows what to do when we get on the island. We went over that on Monday in the staff meeting. I just want to remind you to have fun. This party is as much for you as the politicians, even though I am paying you overtime to be here. But seriously, you've worked hard and I thank you. Relax and enjoy yourselves. If you have fun, so will our guests."

Once on the island, the staff went to their assigned duties. Connie found she had little to do. After checking last minute details with Janie, she climbed the rise to the old lighthouse. This was the highest point on the island and provided a spectacular view. It had been the ideal spot to locate a lighthouse, ships sailing to and from Southport could mark the channel by its beam.

How beautiful it is here, she thought, as she did every time she came. She could see the turbulence of Corncake Inlet, where the Cape Fear River met the Atlantic Ocean. Small choppy waves of river intersected strong currents of ocean, causing a continual band of whitecaps. Tricky waters for boaters, she knew.

The land was as fascinating as the water. Trees and shrubs, bent by years of storms and wind, leaned away from the ocean; branches stretched out like the arms of widows moaning for their lost sailors. The sand had become glaringly hot. Sand pipers and seagulls scurried about, unmindful of how it would scorch human feet. Connie was glad her guests would have tents—and plenty of ice.

This is right, she thought. *It's right to develop this beauty, to let future generations live and vacation here. Humans will always need a place to rest their souls. And by building to protect the land and wildlife, we leave it as pristine as we found it.*

The guests began debarking at one o'clock. Pauline and Sims DuVall were among the first arrivals. Sims helped his wife down the boat ramp with newfound pride. He held Pauline's elbow and escorted her as if she were Scarlet O'Hara dancing at Tara.

Today Pauline was wearing a hot pink shorts outfit decorated with large white sailboats. It clashed with her hair and accentuated her size. The ubiquitous fake pearls nestled in the rolls of fat around her neck. *I'll have to take Pauline shopping,* thought Connie. *I could help her buy clothes to minimize her size. And maybe give her a few hints on weight control.*

As the DuValls rushed toward her, Connie remembered her first impression of the couple. Now they had become dear friends. "Connie, dear. Thank you for inviting us to your lovely party," gushed Pauline. "We're so honored. The island is beautiful and your decorations so tasteful."

"Pauline, Sims, welcome." Connie kissed each one on the cheek. "I wanted to share this day with my friends. And I especially hoped the members of the restoration committee could hear Father Benson speak. Though I doubt Joshua Dunn will be here."

"Oh, pooh. That cold fish." Pauline made Connie laugh by puckering her great lips to imitate a fish blowing bubbles. Pauline lowered her voice to whisper, "I'll be eating just a teensy-weensy bit of your delicious food. And maybe one little glass of wine. I'm on a diet. Simsy loves the new me."

Connie hugged her friend's great girth. Pauline was as big as ever.

Robin and Burly Peters followed the DuValls off the *Wisteria*. The speakers had been asked to arrive early. Connie's heart leapt when she saw Robin. *How handsome he is,* she thought. The anger she had felt earlier melted, leaving a sad, lonely void in its place.

"Connie." He acknowledged her with a curt nod. "Everything is lovely." Then he turned to follow the DuValls to the refreshment stand. She could read nothing in his demeanor. He was certainly short with her. Was he angry, or just hurt?

Burly embraced her in one of his famous teddy bear hugs. "Let's talk later," he whispered.

Guests arrived for the next two hours. Connie had invited Wayne Bailey and Marty Connors. She was sorry that neither could attend. Joe Johnston had brought his wife and introduced her with obvious pride.

The Edmonds staff was kept busy serving the guests and showing them around the island. Dilcey and Ben had been engaged to help. Ben had been disappointed when told that he could not serve guests with Petey the snake wrapped around his shoulders.

Tom Crouton had positioned himself in front of several large drawn-to-scale diagrams of plans for Turtle Nest. He cornered anyone who would listen, promoting his company's development of the island.

"Good work, Tom," Connie murmured as she passed him.

"I'm getting nothing but terrific vibes, Con. The politicians are impressed with our stylistic designs and plans to preserve the environment."

"Me too, Tom. Two senators have asked about buying property for themselves."

The hot summer day reached its peak, then slowly began to wane into the afternoon. Connie enjoyed visiting with her guests, but avoided conversation with Robin.

"Connie, it's quarter to four," Janie sidled up to her boss and whispered in her ear. "I'm going to start assembling everyone for our program."

"It's time, Janie. Are our speakers here? I've seen Father Benson, but how about Bill Pace?"

"He's over there talking to your friend Lucy James and her husband." Janie pointed toward the threesome standing beneath an old water oak.

Lucy was dressed in a smashing yellow linen shorts outfit. With her raven-black hair, she looked like a tiny goldfinch hopping excitedly from one foot to another. "Connie," she called. "You must come meet Bill Pace. He's the wildlife and environment expert who's speaking today."

Connie hurried toward her guests and shook hands with a tall, boyish-looking young man. "Mr. Pace. Welcome. I'm Connie Edmonds. Lucy's told me a great deal about you and your work—all glowing, I assure you."

"Please call me Bill. Yes. Lucy's an avid supporter of our programs, especially the turtle reclamation project."

"Do you know the Loggerheads are an endangered species, Connie?" Lucy interjected. "Bill was telling me that these four-wheel drive vehicles—one tire can crush a nest containing over a hundred eggs. And baby turtles get confused when they see lighted houses and think they're heading toward the ocean. Instead, they die in the sand."

"Well, we won't have any of that on Turtle Nest, will we?" Connie said. "Let me escort Bill to the speaker's stand. Unless you're giving the speech for him."

"Sorry," Lucy giggled. "I do go a bit overboard."

Janie welcomed everyone to the island and recognized Connie as their hostess. The guests applauded in appreciation of the lovely party. Connie even received a few wolf whistles. Bill Pace spoke at length about his department's efforts for plant and wildlife conservation. With the skill of a polished orator, he advertised the Edmonds Company's efforts to protect the environment on Turtle Nest while promoting his own pet projects. When Robin spoke, Connie stood at a distance and listened. She could barely hear him, but saw that the priest had again transported an audience to the Southport of 130 years earlier.

Since her argument with Robin, Connie had thought a great deal about Lucy's insights and Nettie Mae's strange dreams. Was guilt over Amanda Roberts' death keeping her from loving Robin? If so, what should she do about it? Had Suzanne been in love with the Anglican priest? Had her part in John Marshburn's and Rose Greenhow's deaths caused her to believe she was unworthy to love a clergyman? Would Robin ever understand? The last time they were together he'd gone off in a huff. Could she make him see she loved him, but had fears and insecurities that must be considered?

And what of the evidence against Clarence Roberts? At some point she must deal with that. She still held a grudge against Amanda's father. He had stonewalled her for thirty years. There was no way she could forgive that. She had promised Joshua Dunn the evidence would be made public. She intended to keep that promise.

"Help, help! Someone come help. At the pier. A turtle, a poor turtle. I think she's drowning." Connie and her guests turned to see Captain Bob of the *Wisteria* panting up the hill.

"Come. You must come quickly," he gasped. As one body, the party swarmed in the direction indicated by the old sailor.

Bill Pace took the lead and was first to reach the wharf. What he saw broke the heart of the young biologist. A great female Loggerhead thrashed for her life, entwined in fishing line that was wrapped around a piling. As she tired, her head began to sink below the waterline. The swish of her great hind flippers had slowed to a laborious struggle.

Bill knew she would soon die of suffocation. Loggerheads can normally dive for four to five minutes without breathing. They can even rest underwater for several hours at a time. But when under stress, as this one was, they become frightened and lose their ability to hold their breath. That was why so many died each year in shrimp nets or in other fishing gear.

Since it was low tide, Bill could not reach her from the dock. He shouted to Connie. "A small boat. Do you have a small boat on the island?"

As Connie shook her head, Captain Bob rushed up. "There's the lifeboats on the '*Teria*. If you'll give me a hand, we can lower one and save her. I have a knife to cut her free." Bill, Captain Bob, and several men boarded the *Wisteria* to retrieve a lifeboat.

Connie's heart sank as she realized the time it would take to lower the boat and maneuver it to the giant turtle. She watched with the rest of the guests as the reptile's struggles became ever more feeble. Now its great shell floated on top of the water, rapidly drying in the sun. The flippers barely moved, the ancient head rarely surfaced for air. The lifeboat still hung above the water, ensnared in its own lines as precious seconds ticked by.

"She's not going to make it," someone cried. "She's quit moving altogether."

"Oh yes she is!" Connie saw the flash of wild black hair and yellow linen shorts leap into the water. Lucy James splashed beside the turtle and swam to face her. With one tiny hand she forced the great head above the water and held it there.

Lucy treaded water as she supported the leathery creature. Connie held her breath. The turtle could drown Lucy. If she were pinned against the pole or trapped under the huge beast, she could die. Connie tried to forget the other creatures in the sea and the barnacles on the pilings, which would shred Lucy's skin. From the corner of her eye she saw Charlie James preparing to go to his wife's aid.

Bill Pace finally arrived in the lifeboat to cut the turtle free. He sawed at the line with a pocketknife. Because of Lucy's efforts, the animal was regaining strength. She continued to struggle, sloshing Lucy and making Bill's job difficult.

"Just a minute, Luce," Bill gasped, "There." With a loud twang, the line snapped free. The Loggerhead took a great gulp of air, turned, and headed toward the open sea. She thanked Lucy for saving her life with a resounding smack from a hind flipper.

"She did it. Lucy saved the turtle!" Connie turned to Robin standing beside her. Throwing her arms around him, she hugged him tightly. "They did it, Robin. Bill and Lucy did it." How wonderful Robin felt—how warm, safe, and secure.

Then she remembered she shouldn't be holding him. Looking into his kind, hurt face, she could only sob. Turning, she ran down the dock and away from her party.

Chapter 25

Wise Counsel

Connie leaned against Old Baldy and cried. When she was exhausted and had no more tears, she leaned against the old lighthouse in misery. Far below she heard her party gain strength and become ever more festive. Janie, Tom, and the rest of her staff had everything under control.

Twilight settled over the island. Cool breezes began blowing, making the temperature more tolerable. The salt-laden wind stung her face, drying the tears like a veil against her cheeks. Above her, millions of stars began to appear to light the evening sky. Connie thought of sailors who had used the stars and her old lighthouse to guide them to safe port. How she wished she had a guide to steer her on a steady course.

"So there you are. Your staff said this was a favorite spot for you." The warm, softly modulated voice of Burly Peters caressed the night air.

"Oh Burly, forgive me." Connie started to rise. "I'm being a terrible hostess. Are you enjoying yourself?"

"Sit, Connie, sit." The bishop dropped to the sand beside her. "It's a wonderful party. I had to take a break, though. Pauline DuVall has danced my legs off. She and Sims have invented a new dance—the Turtle Trot."

In spite of her misery, Connie smiled. "Ah, Pauline."

Burly took her white hand in his two large black ones. "Connie, what's wrong?"

"Nothing, Burly. As you said, the party's going fine. We even had added entertainment when Lucy saved the turtle. I could never have staged that."

"Don't hedge. You've been miserable all evening, moping around and not acting like yourself. Look at you now. You don't run away crying from a party that's the social success of the season, if everything is fine."

Connie understood why the man was a bishop. Beyond his soothing voice and warm touch, there was a gentleness about his very presence that brought peace. Just being near him calmed her. She imagined he'd stood by many sick or sorrowing parishioners and brought the same comfort.

"Oh Burly," Connie began. "I've made such a mess of my life."

"Judging by this party, that's not true. I'd say the Turtle Nest development is a sure thing."

"Oh, business is fine. Couldn't be better. But I can't seem to keep my personal life on course."

"Let me guess. Robin Benson."

"Among other things. But mostly Robin."

"Connie, forgive me for being blunt. But let's get straight to the point. Lucy and Robin have come to me, on their own and at different times. Both are insightful people. Both are worried. In addition to being in love with you, Robin is a priest. It's his business to know when someone is hurting. Lucy has shared some of your history when you were recruits in the Army. Given that background, do you want to pick up the story?"

A sharp pang of anger flashed through Connie. "They had no right—" she began.

"They had every right. They care about you."

Connie shrugged. What was the use? Lucy did things her own way. Like today with the turtle. That was why Connie loved her. If she confided in Burly it was, as he said, out of concern. As for Robin, she didn't know. She was too emotionally exhausted to figure that one out.

"Did Lucy tell you about Amanda Roberts' suicide?" Connie asked.

"Yes."

"Did she tell you her theory that I won't let myself love anyone, especially a priest, because of it?"

"Yes."

"And what did Robin say?"

"That he loved you. That you said you loved him. That he'd asked you to marry him, but you didn't want to be a clergyman's wife. He said he accused you of thinking you were too good to marry a priest. He realizes that was wrong and is sorry."

"What do you think, Burly? Am I afraid to love Robin because of Amanda? Lucy says marrying a priest is like marrying God. Am I really afraid of God?"

"Maybe. I've seen similar situations. But you must remember. Robin is not God. He will make mistakes. I think he's told you that he wrestles daily with his temper. He lost it the other night when you didn't give him an immediate 'yes.'

"He should have given you time to think about his marriage proposal. But knowing Robin, I'd say the asking took all his courage. And his ego was probably hurt. We men, even those of us who are priests, do cling to our egos."

Connie sat in silence, pondering the bishop's words. She finally understood that Robin wrestled his own demons, just as she did. Somehow, that made her love him more.

She knew then that she must tell the whole story. "There's more, Burly. More about another religion entirely—old slave beliefs."

"I never said the Episcopal Church was the only way."

Connie told him about Nettie Mae's strange dreams and Suzanne Marshburn's warning. The bishop sat quietly, considering what she'd said. Finally he spoke, "What a lot of coincidences."

"It gets worse, Burly. My involvement with Amanda Roberts didn't end with her death. Really, that's when it began. Her father is Senator Clarence Roberts. All these years he's held me responsible for his daughter's death and for the cover-up that followed. Much of what he says is true. But I was eighteen, away from home for the first time, anxious to get ahead. I wouldn't make the same mistakes today.

"For years Clarence Roberts has hounded me with the memory of the suicide. Roberts has tried to block every important business deal I've ever made. He even planted Joshua Dunn as a mole on the restoration committee to stymie our progress. Remember how opposed Dunn was to the continuation of restoration after the discovery of the slave bones? And the debate over rebuilding the foundation? That was Roberts at work. Dunn was just his mouthpiece."

"Are you sure? Those are strong accusations to make."

"Oh, I'm sure. I've been dealing with Roberts so long I know his handiwork. But now I have the goods on Clarence Roberts. I have enough evidence to destroy him and his reputation. History will judge the senator harshly."

"What do you mean?" asked Burly.

"I've spent a great deal of time and money researching the senator's past. It's quite shady, criminal really. There's enough to make Roberts the laughing stock of North Carolina, probably the entire nation. That is, if he's not indicted on criminal charges.

"Roberts wants to call a truce, even wants me to help him lobby for federal laws to protect recruits in the military. But I'm releasing my report to the press on Monday. The treatment Roberts will get from the public will make him wish he was a buck private being berated by his sergeant. He'd like to get off that easily."

Until that moment, Connie had been undecided as to when, and how, she would use the evidence against Roberts. This was as good a time as any. Better to move on than to wallow in indecision.

She was out of breath when she finished. It occurred to her to wonder why she'd confessed to the bishop rather than Marty Connors. Maybe it was his warm presence or maybe she was tired of carrying the burden alone.

Burly sat quietly beside her, his shoulders hunched from the weight of what she'd said. Finally he mumbled, "Evil begets evil."

"What did you say?"

"Connie. You must understand." The bishop was not visible in the darkness, but she could hear the gravity in his voice. She knew he faced her. "I would be remiss as a man of God if I didn't tell you this. Believe me. I admire and respect you, as much as anyone I know. Perhaps that's why I'm even bringing this up.

"You must not turn the report over to the press. It will only continue the awful harm that's already been done. Your happiness depends on it. Probably your very soul. Don't you see? The wickedness began when some hotshot female drill sergeant decided to make life miserable for a privileged young girl. It's perpetuated itself for thirty years through the senator's meanness to you. Now you're planning to carry on the evil by printing questionable and damning material. That will make you no better than Roberts.

"I may be a bishop, but there are lots of things I don't know about the afterlife. I figure I'll find out about that soon enough. But I do know this. There's always a price to pay, whether in this life or in the next. Look at you. You're paying the price now. You're miserable. You obviously love Robin, but can't bring yourself to marry him. From what you've told me of Suzanne Marshburn, she's still paying a price. Her spirit's not at rest, even though she died a century ago."

"So I'm supposed to let Roberts continue to harass me?" In the darkness Burly heard Connie's voice rise in indignation.

"No. Let him know you have the report, and that you'll use it if necessary. There's probably enough truth in it to silence him forever. It may not matter anyway. Roberts is not expected to live much longer.

"As to whether or not you decide to help him pass strict laws governing the military, that's your decision. It's immaterial. What does matter is that you and Roberts quit playing this silly cat and mouse game. It's made him an evil, calculating old man. And you're headed in the same direction.

"You've been so focused on defeating Roberts and building your business. Soften up now and accept Robin's love—and God's."

"You're wrong, Burly. I've built my business by being strong. I don't back down. I'll go to the paper on Monday. I have an appointment with Marty Connors at ten o'clock. Right after that, I intend to go to the *Pilot* with my research. Clarence Roberts will be front page news in Thursday's first edition."

Bishop Peters sat with Connie a while longer. He said nothing else. Finally, he squeezed her hand and vanished into the darkness.

After Burly left, Connie continued to rest against the lighthouse. She was too tired to think of what he'd said, much less make sense of it. Her party was beginning to wind down. She must make an appearance. The guests would be looking for her. She could lose important votes for Turtle Nest if she didn't say her good-byes. When she was certain the red blotches had faded from her cheeks, she left the lighthouse for her dying party.

Chapter 26

Copper Coins

Connie woke the next morning with a dull, nagging headache. She moped around her cottage in a kind of fog. Exhausted from yesterday's celebration, she was also elated. Turtle Nest would become a reality. She was certain of it.

Katie sensed her sluggishness and avoided her. "You should be a dog," Connie hissed. "A dog would show me some sympathy instead of ignoring me." Katie glared at her in disgust and went to swat bugs in the sunshine.

By early afternoon the walls of the home she loved began to close in on her. *I've got to get out,* she thought. Leaving the house, she had no sense of direction, but strolled through the town without purpose.

The temperature had climbed to ninety-six degrees that afternoon, but wandering the streets of the sleepy village, Connie didn't feel the heat. Old oaks, magnolias, and dogwoods shaded lawns and sidewalks. The crepe myrtle was in full summer bloom, bursting out in white, red, or watermelon, depending on the tree.

Connie thought again about how glad she was that she had settled in Southport—quiet and old and ripe with tradition, but close to the business hubs of Wilmington and even Raleigh. And Brunswick County was growing. She had no doubt she was positioned to capitalize on an upcoming real estate boom. Retirees, young families, professionals, all were coming to appreciate the beauty of the area.

Already her head had cleared as she strolled the sidewalks. She was ready to resume her life. She would finish her walk down Main Street, then double back for home.

At the end of the road, Connie noticed a dirt path she had never seen before. Low-hanging branches hid the street name. *Birch Street* she read, brushing aside a limb. Feeling adventuresome, she walked on. It was still early and she could use the extra exercise.

At first, the overhanging branches were cool and inviting. Gardenias grew tall along the way. Their perfume hung heavy in the air—pleasant, but somewhat cloying. Shadows crossed and criss-crossed the path, stretching long fingers toward her. As she walked, the shadows turned to inky darkness. The temperature plummeted twenty degrees, wind whipped the treetops.

Like a fish snared by a line, Connie was drawn into the gloom. Her heart raced, yet she was powerless to turn back. Unfamiliar insects, cicadas perhaps, played to a thunderous crescendo, then ceased abruptly. The woods were deathly quiet, until they again sounded their strange chorus.

Connie tripped, then regained her footing. *This is foolish,* she thought. *I'm a grown woman. Yet I'm terrified.* Just as she willed herself to retrace her steps, she stumbled into hot, bright sunshine.

Connie stepped into the dirt yard of a tumbled down cabin. *Unbelievable,* she thought. *This looks like a farmyard, right in the middle of Southport.* Chickens scratched the dirt, a rooster strutted to impress them, an old dog snored in the sun. The scene was from the dustbowl of *The Grapes of Wrath*, rather than the affluent 1970s.

"Why was I so scared?" she wondered aloud. She turned to the path she had just left. It had disappeared.

"Girlie," someone hailed from the cabin. "Girlie, do dat be you?"

Connie saw a small, wizened gnome of a black woman standing on the porch. She supported herself with a huge, gnarled stick. Despite the heat, her head was covered and she wore long, dark rags.

"Girlie, do dat be you?" the gnome croaked. "Do dat be Helen's girl come to see me?"

Nettie Mae. This was Nettie Mae's cabin. Connie remembered her mother had said she lived at the end of Birch Street.

What did she do now? She was in no mood to discuss ghosts, voodoo, or dreams. But it would be incredibly rude to ignore the old woman. She continued calling, waving her arms and pounding the porch with her stick. And Connie still couldn't find the path.

"Yes ma'am. It's me. I'm Connie Edmonds. Helen Edmonds' daughter." She approached the bent figure and peered beneath the hood. The face was strangely familiar.

"You done come. You want to know 'bout my dreams. Come in de house, child." Nettie Mae extended a draped arm, pointing toward the house.

Again, Connie could think of no reason to refuse. "Well, maybe for a minute."

It took Connie's eyes several minutes to adjust to the dark interior after the bright sunlight. Chairs, tables, an oil stove were vague shapes as her pupils slowly focused. From the next room, Donald Duck chastised his nephews for dousing him with water from the garden hose.

Nettie Mae shouted into the other room. "Turn dat damn thing down! I done got com'ny." Connie heard a grunt, a shuffle, and blessed lowered volume. Her hostess steered her to the chair and pushed her into it. The old woman was surprisingly strong. Connie looked around. The room was small, but meticulously clean. Lime green linoleum covered the floor, stopping only when it abutted the stove. A black velvet picture of Elvis Presley hung on the opposite wall. Beside it hung—"Oh my God," gasped Connie. Her hands flew to her face as adrenaline drove her from the chair. Panicked, she bolted for the door.

Hanging next to Elvis, the copper necklace—the jewelry of her nightmare. The necklace seemed to leer at her, wicked and menacing. In a flash, Connie realized why Nettie looked familiar—she bore a striking resemblance to the dream demon of her nightmares.

Connie groped for the screen door. But the dog that had snored harmlessly in the yard now guarded the exit with bared yellow teeth. Slobber drooled from its lips and it emitted a low, menacing growl.

Nettie Mae's hand enclosed her arm in a vise-like grip. "Where you be going, girl? You came here on your own 'cord. Now you be running off. You ain't gone do dat."

Connie felt terror ice down her back and pool at the base of her spine. For some moments she stood trembling, barred in front by the dog and in back by an old woman half her size.

Her voice, when it returned, was hoarse with fright. "The necklace. Where did you get the necklace?"

"What you talking 'bout?"

"The necklace on the wall. Beside Elvis. The one made of copper."

"Dat old thing? Dat were Alethia's. My great-aunt. She be dead more'n fifty year. Dat necklace can't hurt you, girl."

Connie was too weak to resist as Nettie Mae led her back to the chair. Her legs gave way as she dropped onto the cushion. Again she looked at the necklace. It did look harmless, overpowered by the King of Rock and Roll. But Connie had seen it when it had a life of its own, jangling from the neck of the she-witch.

"You best talk to me, girl. Something's done skairt you good. You best tell me what it be." Nettie Mae's tone revealed nothing. Connie didn't know if she were sympathetic, threatening, or just curious.

Connie's voice had regained none of its normal volume. When she spoke, she sounded raspy and restrained. "The necklace. I've seen it before. In nightmares. Around the neck of a demon."

Nettie Mae remained quiet for some moments. Finally she whispered, "So dat be it."

"I beg your pardon?"

"Dat 'splains it. Strange things been happening 'round here. Joe told you 'bout my dreams. But dere be more. I done had other dreams. Dreams 'bout Alethia. And she's wearing dat necklace. She brought dat with her from Afrika. Wore it all de time.

"And dere's done been other things. I done had chickens die for no reason. Yesterday I burned my hand real bad. I never do dat. And Bubba," she jerked her head toward the other room. "He done came home after more'n twenty year. Something be afoot, I says."

"Tell me about your dreams of Alethia. Are they frightening? Mine always are." In spite of her desire to distance herself from the supernatural, Connie needed answers.

Nettie Mae continued her discourse. "It's Alethia. Her spirit's here 'bouts. She's undead. I knowed she'd come back. I knowed dat one would."

"What do you mean?"

Nettie Mae turned on her with vehemence. "You don't need know nothing else, white girl. You go on home. Quit sticking your nose in my bus'ness."

Connie's spine stiffened as she faced the small woman with renewed purpose. "No. I won't. I won't go home. I want some answers. You invited me here. You told Joe I could come whenever I wanted. You brought me in your home. And your dog won't let me leave.

"I want to know what this is all about. I want to know why your great-aunt appears in my dreams. And why that terrifies you."

Nettie Mae slumped into a rickety wooden chair. The fierce Lilliputian had shrunk, fragile as a dried cornhusk. Her clothes enveloped her like a death shroud. She didn't answer for several minutes. Connie held her ground, she could outwait the old woman.

"Awright. I'll tell you. You has de right. But don't you ever be telling Joe."

"Joe?"

"Ma great-grandson. You must never tell him dis. It would kill him. He be a good man. He don't need to know bad stuff 'bout his kin."

"I won't tell Joe. I seldom see him, anyway."

"And dere's one more thing." Nettie Mae began seeing possibilities in the situation.

"What's that?"

"I ain't gone live much longer. I want to be buried in dat cemetery. I want to be buried wif dem slaves. Deys my people. Dat's where I want to lie."

"I could talk to Father Benson. It's possible. Maybe you could have a grave beside them, with a nice marker."

"Dat'd be awright."

"Now tell me about Alethia."

Nettie could think of no more bribes, so began her story. "Alethia's loose awright. I bets when you see her, you be wfh some man. Right?"

Connie blushed, in spite of herself. Nettie Mae rushed on without waiting for an answer.

"Alethia were like dat. She couldn't have her man. So she don't want nobody else have deirs, neither. She done dis afore. But sometimes she be trying to warn you, too. Sometimes she be trying to help. I never can figger dat one out."

"What do you mean?"

Nettie Mae sighed and slowly shook her head. "Alethia love John Marshburn. I don't know why. He were mean and cruel. But she did. I guess dere's no 'splaining love. Alethia done spent de last hundred years scaring people or warning dem."

"But John Marshburn mistreated his slaves. He abused them and whipped them."

"Dat a fact. Dat how he died. Beatin' a slave. Dat slave were Alethia. And she were eight months along. Wif his child."

"Oh, Lord" whispered Connie.

"Dere's more. You might's well know de whole story, if you gone know part."

"How do you know so much? It happened long ago."

Again Nettie sighed. "Alethia won't my great-aunt. I made dat up 'cause I were shame. She were my grandmother. Dat baby she were carr'ing, it were my mother. I heared her and my mother hollering 'bout it one night. When I were jist a li'l girl. Dey didn't think I heared, but I did."

"So that's what you don't want Joe to find out, that John Marshburn was his great-great-great grandfather."

"Dat be part of it. But dat not be all. Alethia were evil. She were beau'ful, but she were evil."

"What do you mean?"

"She kilt John Marshburn. She and Suzanne."

Connie leaned against the cushions of the old chair. Thoughts and images swirled through her brain. Because of Nettie Mae's dialect, she had difficulty following the fantastic story. Yet she had to know how it ended.

"Alethia and Suzanne both killed John Marshburn? How could that be?"

"It were like your mama thought. At least part of it. Suzanne's pa did get de pisin from Alethia. But not 'nuff to kill him. Alethia didn't want him daid, she just want him to be mad at Suzanne.

But Captain Cogdill didn't know dat. And he had to leave afore he could give the pisin to Marshburn. He told Suzanne to do it. Suzanne put some in John's wine, but not 'nuff.

"John stomped out of the big house hollering, 'That's the worse wine I've ever tasted. Are you trying to poison me?'" Strangely, when Nettie Mae quoted others, she adopted their speech and mannerisms. Now she preened like an angry gentleman farmer. Her voice had lost its dialect and dropped an octave.

"He went down to Alethia's cabin. He always went dere when he were mad. 'Come here and give me some cunt, gal,' he ordered. 'Your black pussy ain't as good as Suzanne's, but it'll do. After this baby's born, I'm selling it down river. I won't have no nigger baby hanging on your tits when I want 'em. And you better never get yourself knocked up again. I'm sick of screwing you from the rear.'

"Alethia start crying. She had want a baby so long. Dis were de first time she ever be preg'ant. Now Marshburn say she can't keep it. And she knew he love Suzanne. Alethia were a queen in Afrika. She were dirt to John Marshburn.

"After he finish wif her, he told Alethia to get him more wine. She get it, but she put in more pisin. She couldn't let him sell her baby. And she didn't want him to go back to Suzanne.

"'This is awful,'" he hollered. "'Can't get good wine from my wife or my whore.' He be pig-eye mad. Alethia don't have on no clothes, but he grab her and drag her to the whupping tree. Dat's when he die. He hit her one lick and he fall down dead.

"My mother were born the next month. Alethia love de baby, but she grieve for John Marshburn. One night when she were drunk, she told Mammy all 'bout it. Said ev'ryone thought it were his heart. 'Cept for Suzanne. Suzanne thought she done kilt him."

"What you doing, Ma? Who you be talking to?"

In spite of herself, Connie gasped. A caricature of a man stood framed in the doorway—the television viewer from the other room. His face resembled a candle left to burn itself out. The nose and mouth slid down like cold tallow, bunching together at the chin. The blank stare promised little intelligence. One side of the deformed body was that of a 250-pound giant. The other half belonged to a man half the size.

"Dis be Bubba," Nettie Mae said. "Ain't pretty, are he? Now you know de rest of my story. Bubba are my son. His daddy were my oldest brother. He rape me when I were twelve. De meanness didn't die with John Marshburn. Just please don't tell Joe."

Chapter 27

Sermons in Glass

Connie's week had been so amazing, she was not surprised when she dressed for church the next morning. Why not? Everything she thought she knew or understood had been refuted. Why not become completely bizarre and go hear Robin preach?

Upon entering the church, she noted the beginning stages of restoration. Like a proud mother, she admired the expert refinishing of century old pews. The ceiling appeared bare since removal of the flags for cleaning. Soon they would parade in their rightful place, high above the faithful.

She sat halfway down the middle, on the left. Slipping easily into the routine of the service, she mouthed words known by rote since childhood. Connie remembered Sundays of pressing her knees deep into the prayer cushions. Each week she'd strive to make a larger dent. *I certainly wasn't paying attention*, she thought.

Robin began the service with no indication that he had noticed her. Connie suffered through the prayers, the Gospel, the Psalms. *How irrelevant*, she thought. *None of this affects my life today.*

She tried to listen to the sermon. After all, that was why she had come, to hear Robin preach. His beautiful, melodious voice filled the sanctuary, but her mind wandered to the previous day. Though fantastic, Connie was sure of the truth of Nettie Mae's story. The old woman had no reason to lie.

Connie had left after she met Bubba. As she said good-bye, Nettie Mae took the copper necklace from the wall. "Take this wif you," she whispered, forcing the jewelry into Connie's hand. "It's the onliest way you'll ever be free of her. If you got de necklace, you got Aletheia. Otherwise, she gone haint you fo'ever."

Connie had shrunk from the talisman. "What'll I do with it? I don't want it."

"You'll know when de time come."

".... so the Nazi guards separated families. The ones who could work stood behind the fence, watching the helpless march to the gas chambers. One little fellow screamed in anguish. His mother couldn't bear it. Her life, and that of her husband, had been spared. But her son was terrified. She slipped through the barbed wire and lifted the little boy. Immediately, he stopped crying and nestled in his mother's arms. The husband pleaded for his wife to return. But she entered the chamber, carrying her child.

"My friends, this is a true story. A sad one, but I tell it to illustrate a point. God's love is like that of the mother's. He has promised to be with us. Even unto the ends of the earth.

"That's what love is, be it divine, maternal, or between man and wife. A promise to be there. Even unto death."

Connie caught just enough of the sermon to hear Robin's graphic story. His words made her understand the child's fear and the mother's compassion. She thought of little else through the rest of the service.

As they said final prayers, she was tempted to play her old game of press-the-prayer-cushion. Instead, she searched for a more adult focus. The stained glass window beside her was lovely. Usually the flags hid it. Today the sun shone through, illuminating the colors and characters of the design.

This window showed the Virgin Mary praying at her son's crucifixion. Though inanimate, Mary's face portrayed faith and hope. How was that possible? How could Mary watch her son endure so much cruelty and pain? How could she see her son die, yet experience hope?

Connie left the church with her questions unanswered. Slipping out the side door, she avoided Robin. Today, shaking hands and making small talk did not appeal to her.

Chapter 28

Insights

Connie's appointment with Marty Connors was at ten o'clock. Driving the sleepy Monday morning streets, she pondered the upcoming session. Usually Marty asked about her life during the previous week—her thoughts, her dreams, any insights.

So much had happened this week. More than she could cram into a one-hour session. Suzanne's letters, her visit to Nettie Mae, the Turtle Nest Party, Robin's marriage proposal and church service—all major life events. Where should she focus?

She was tired of rehashing thoughts of Robin and Clarence Roberts. She'd done that with Burly. Despite his advice, Connie had no answers for the dilemma of Robin, but was determined to go public with her report on Roberts.

The common thread in the extraordinary happenings of the past few weeks was Suzanne Marshburn. Connie had long sensed parallels between her own life and that of Suzanne's. She and Marty had never explored this link.

The connection strengthened as she told Robin of Suzanne's last letter. She had become Suzanne, felt her pain, taken her voice. Nettie Mae, too, sensed the bond between the two women. In dreams and visions Suzanne appeared to the insightful old crone with messages for Connie.

"Oh yes," the counselor assured her when she broached the subject. "Connections with events and people of former times exist. Again, I believe these work for our good. A benevolent force, greater than us all, dredges history then spews out the findings. Sort of like a miner panning for gold.

"Some therapists get off on former lives and reincarnation. I don't go that far. But I've seen too many instances of the past affecting the present not to believe in its influence. And in every instance the ultimate goal is the patient's happiness and well-being. I can't explain, I just accept."

As usual, Marty gave Connie her full attention. The therapist said she listened with her third ear, two ears to hear the conversation and a third attuned to nuances and insights.

The office hadn't changed since the first time that Connie had come to see Marty. The boar's head still glared from the wall, the still dogs slept comfortably—one in her lap and the other on its bed. Marty still wore outrageous make-up and clothes. Connie drew strength from this familiarity. In Marty she had gained a trusted friend and wise counselor.

Connie told what she'd learned of Suzanne Marshburn's history—her part in the death of her husband and in the drowning of Rose Greenhow.

She described the note found in her mother's chest. The one Suzanne wrote damning her actions. Maybe for one of the deaths, maybe both. They would never know. But just as Connie shouldered blame for Amanda Roberts' suicide, Suzanne also harbored tremendous guilt.

Possibly Suzanne, too, had suffered a mental breakdown. Connie remembered the reference in Captain Cogdill's diary to his daughter's stay at the York Hospital. At one point the captain had even labeled Suzanne "insane."

"That would fit the timeline," Marty acknowledged. "Your Suzanne was fortunate to be admitted to the York Hospital. William Tuke of England was a pioneer in humane treatment of the mentally ill. Before his time 'mad' persons were starved, beaten, tortured as witches, restrained in dungeons and attics.

"Patients at the York Hospital received good nutrition and engaged in useful chores. Another technique used was pet therapy. You've met my two pups. It's hard to feel anxiety with Bojo snoring over there on his bed.

"Your Suzanne Marshburn was probably part of this scene. As I've told you, she was fortunate. Many institutions in Europe and the United States still held antiquated views on treatment of mental diseases.

"Suzanne lived before the work of Sigmund Freud. As you probably know, Freud's work began the science of psychoanalysis. He proved mental affliction was just that, an illness. This furthered the belief that such people could be helped and deserved compassion. But prejudices linger."

"Do you think Suzanne's apparent breakdown could have been similar to mine," Connie asked. "Caused by self-blame?"

"Probably. The important thing is what you do with that knowledge. What do you know of Suzanne's life after she was hospitalized? You say she's appeared to Nettie Mae with a warning for you. What sense do you make of that?"

"Well," Connie began. "Suzanne's message was 'Don't waste time blaming yourself for another's death. I did. And I regret it', or something to that affect.

"As for her life after her breakdown, Captain Cogdill wrote that one of Suzanne's few visitors was a Reverend Thaddeus Hepplewhite. Other friends and relatives stayed away. They believed Suzanne contagious. But Reverend Hepplewhite seemed fond of Suzanne. At one point the captain hoped for a marriage. But it never happened."

"There you have it," Marty summarized. "A message from beyond. Suzanne experienced humane treatment. She was lucky for that. But she didn't enjoy the benefits you have—medication, counseling, acceptance of your breakdown as unavoidable, and not a weakness on your part.

"I'd say Suzanne is trying to tell you to get on with your life. She was undoubtedly cloistered by her father, shunned by many, filled with self doubt. You live in a more enlightened society. Suzanne is encouraging you to use that to your advantage."

As Connie left the session, Marty grabbed her arm. "Hey. Tell me again Suzanne's full name."

"Suzanne Cogdill Marshburn."

Marty pondered, then laughed her loud guffaw. "Wouldn't that be a coincidence? A Suzanne Cogdill worked with Dorothea Dix until Dix's death in 1887." When Connie gave her a puzzled look, Marty explained.

"Dorothea Dix was an American woman who led the drive to build state hospitals for the mentally ill. She visited a Massachusetts house of correction in 1841, and returned shocked at the treatment of mental patients. Dix campaigned for her cause until she was eighty.

"A younger woman, Suzanne Cogdill, became her assistant around 1877. Cogdill worked in the South, but always gave credit to Miss Dix. Our own Dix Hill, the state mental hospital in Raleigh, was named for Dorothea Dix. That's where you were almost sent before you admitted yourself to Dosher."

"Wow." Connie whooped. "This story is a web of coincidences. Maybe Suzanne returned to the States and worked with Miss Dix. Perhaps in her brush with mental illness, Suzanne saw how poorly patients were treated and desired change. My friend, Lucy James, says doing for others helps absolve our own guilt. Maybe Suzanne found that to be true."

"Perhaps that's what happened," said Marty. "Perhaps Suzanne used her guilt over her role in her husband and friend's deaths for good. Perhaps that gave her peace."

Chapter 29

Endings

After leaving Marty Connors, Connie drove to the newspaper office and entered the lobby of the *Southport Pilot,* the thick packet damning Clarence Roberts tucked under her arm. She approached the young receptionist whose badge said that her name was Betsy. "Where's the editor in chief's office?" Connie asked, trying to hide the nervousness in her voice.

She started toward the door Betsy indicated. As she did, a lanky male figure unfolded and stood beside her.

"Robin! What are you doing here?" Connie's face flushed in surprise.

"Burly Peters said you might need me this morning. So I came." Robin slipped his arm around her.

"Did he tell you why I'm here?"

"Yes. Burly is my spiritual advisor as well as my bishop and friend. Priests need counseling as much as lay people, maybe more so. He said he didn't agree with what you are doing, but that you might need my support."

"What else did he say?"

"He made me understand that if I loved you, which I do, I should come. So I'm here. I want to be with you for the rest of my life. I think I could be a good husband. I'm working on controlling my temper. With Burly's help, I'm making progress."

"Burly didn't tell you what's in this report?"

"No. And I really don't care. If it's part of you, it's part of me."

"Even if it's wrong? You love me enough to be here even if what I'm doing is wrong?"

"Hey. Didn't you hear my sermon yesterday? Wasn't that Connie Edmonds in the congregation? Love isn't about who's right and who's wrong. It's about being there when your loved one needs you. And I figure you need me right now."

"Mortalizing," Connie whispered.

"What's that?"

"Mortalizing. It's a term Dilcey uses. It means God being involved in our daily life. You're talking about mortalizing."

She finally understood—the message of the sermon, the stained glass, Robin's presence today. Just like Mary at her son's crucifixion and the Jewish mother at the gas chamber, Robin came because he loved her.

Connie tucked the thick report into her bag. She no longer felt the need, or even the desire, for vindication against Roberts. The evidence was there if she ever needed it.

She wanted to get on with her life, not spend it rehashing the past. Amanda was dead, Suzanne was dead, Alethia was dead. She'd let these ghosts lie and not perpetuate the evil surrounding them.

Robin sensed her lightened mood and tilted her face, caressing her cheek. She stood on tiptoe and kissed him fully on the lips. Betsy and a secretary applauded loudly.

Connie withdrew and took his arm. As she propelled him toward the exit door she waved to the two girls behind the desk.

"I thought you wanted to see the editor in chief," Betsy called.

"Oh. It can wait. I don't have time for that. But I'll be back soon to see the bridal editor." She continued, steering Robin toward the door. And the sunshine of their future.

Epilogue

▼

Robin guided the little boat into mid-channel. Why Connie insisted on going out today was beyond him. A terrible day for sailing, the wind blew from the northeast and a rain squall threatened. Besides, he had work to do.

Connie's mood was unnerving to Robin. She seemed at peace, but any attempt at conversation met with silence or, at best, a monosyllable. This was not his idea of a good time.

"Stop. Stop the boat here, Robin."

"Why here? Let me at least get out of the main channel. A large boat could swamp us."

"No, here. I don't know why. Just stop here. I'll only take a minute."

With that, Connie stood and threw the copper necklace deep into the water. "Rest in peace Amanda, Rose, Suzanne, Alethia," she whispered to no one but the wind.

Women, thought Robin. *Sail all the way out here, then throw a perfectly good necklace in the water.* He'd never understand it but realized he was in for a lifetime of not understanding—and couldn't wait for that lifetime to begin.

Andy's Stuffed Clams

½ stick butter or margarine
½ c. chopped celery
½ c. chopped onions
1 ½ pt. chopped clams
1 (8 oz.) pkg. Pepperidge Farm Herb Stuffing
½ t. salt
pepper to taste
½ c. Parmesan cheese
1 can mushroom soup
2 dashes Worcestershire sauce
Clam juice

Saute butter, onion and celery. Mix all ingredients. Put in clam shell. (If you don't have real shells, make them out of aluminum foil.) Bake at 350 degrees for 15 minutes. Use only enough clam juice to hold stuffing together.

978-0-595-41057-6
0-595-41057-X

Printed in the United States
72081LV00004B/307-348